A Piece of the Sky

David Patneaude

ALBERT WHITMAN & COMPANY
MORTON GROVE, ILLINOIS

—Also by David Patneaude—
Colder Than Ice • *Dark Starry Morning* • *Deadly Drive*
Framed in Fire • *Haunting at Home Plate*
The Last Man's Reward • *Someone Was Watching*

Library of Congress Cataloging-in-Publication Data

Patneaude, David.
A piece of the sky / by David Patneaude ; cover illustration by Layne Johnson.
p. cm.
Summary: Fourteen-year-old Russell, his friend Phoebe, and her brother Isaac
must find a legendary meteor in the Oregon mountains before it is exploited.
ISBN-13: 978-0-8075-6536-0 (hardcover)
[1. Meteorites—Fiction. 2. Mountaineering—Fiction. 3. Oregon—Fiction.]
I. Title.
PZ7.P2734Pie 2007 [Fic]—dc22 2006023529

Design by Carol Gildar.

For information about Albert Whitman & Company,
please visit our web site at www.albertwhitman.com.

To David Bray, who once told me
a real-life tale that kept me up at night,
asking myself, *What if?*

๛ Contents ๛

Chapter One
Matthew: July 20, 1856

Hard ground, morning chill, and mule smells woke Matthew before sunrise. Stiff, cold, and hungry, he longed for his own bed, his mother's voice, her warm, sweet bread. He even missed his brother James's endless questions. But Matthew was far, far from home.

While stars faded into brightening sky, he walked into the deeper woods and relieved himself. When he returned to the campsite, Dr. Evans was sitting up, facing a bald, round-topped mountain in the distance. The night before, when the party had arrived, the mountain had been part of the darkness. Now it looked like a black sun rising over the lumpy horizon.

"How do you think it lost its cover?" the doctor said.

"Its trees, you mean?" Matthew asked.

The doctor stood. His feet were bare, but he still wore

the ankle-length housecoat—a banyan, he called it—that he slept in every night. "Yes. Why are the trees infuriatingly abundant everywhere but on that skull of a mountain?"

Matthew considered the possibilities. Too much sun? Not on the south coast of the Oregon Territory. Too little rain? No. Rain—buckets of it—fell regularly here. The thick growth everywhere, from the carpet of grasses and flowers and mushrooms and moss, to the tips of the tallest firs, was testimony. Suddenly he had a thought: "Indians."

"Indians?"

"Indians set fires to keep brush and trees down. It helps them in their hunting."

"Yes." The doctor's gaze returned to the mountain. "We've seen evidence of that practice on the lower prairies and meadows. But I don't believe Indians are responsible for what we're observing here."

"Rocky ground?" Matthew guessed. "Perhaps the mountain is one giant boulder. The trees would have no place to root and settle in."

"A thoughtful theory, young Matthew. But I think not. These trees seem to grow in the most inhospitable of places. A spoonful of wet dirt is all they need."

Matthew thought hard, searching Dr. Evans's face for

clues. Did this man, who had long studied the earth and its many inhabitants, who had more education than all the settlers of Port Orford combined, expect the answer to come from a thirteen-year-old caretaker of mules? The thought warmed Matthew's insides.

Dr. Evans cleared his throat. His two assistants, Lemieux and Poirier, stirred in their blankets, one of them mumbling sleep-drowned words in unfathomable French. Their slumbering shapes, close by the fire pit, emerged like phantoms in the gathering light.

An answer came to Matthew like a flying ember of burning cedar. "Wildfire?" He looked at the doctor and saw the beginnings of a smile.

"You're learning, Matt. You've looked around, you've taken some cues from nature, you're approaching the solution. But you're not there yet."

Matthew shrugged. He was out of ideas.

The doctor changed the subject. "How many hours until we reach that mountain?" he asked.

Now he expected Matthew to be a guide, a surveyor, a mathematician. But Matthew had spent time in the coastal mountain range. He recognized distances, the encumbrances of undergrowth and terrain, how long it took to navigate them. "I would say this evening, Doctor. If the mules don't balk."

"And we don't waste this fine day standing here and guessing." The doctor went to Lemieux and Poirier and shook them awake. When he looked at Matthew, there was a flame of excitement in his eyes. "Ready the mules, son. We have ground to cover and a mountain with secrets to share."

Chapter Two
Kick Me, I'm in Port Orford:
July 20, Present

I stepped through the front door, soaked with sweat and ocean mist. My lungs felt alive and clean, and I had to admit I liked the feeling. Back in California you never knew what you were breathing. But aside from unpolluted air, I couldn't think of much good to say for Port Orford, the shrimp-sized town on the Oregon coast I'd be calling home for the rest of the summer.

I heard Mom unloading the dishwasher, stacking plates. I peeled off my shoes while my nose filled with the smell of baking. My eyes wandered around Grandpa's living room and I tried to think of a top ten list of good things about Port Orford. I got to five—the air, the scenery, the library, meeting Phoebe, seeing Grandpa.

But even the seeing-Grandpa one had some holes in it. His memory was fading, and fast. He was Grandpa, but not the Grandpa I remembered. He'd lost some of his fire when Grandma died four years earlier, but now the flame was barely flickering. Was there a way to get it rekindled?

Mom had already gotten rid of a lot of his stuff, but across the room, in the center of the mantel, next to his wedding photo, sat one of his untouchables: a shadow box framing a half-drab, half-shiny, bell-shaped chunk of rock the size of a baby's fist. I wasn't sure why the keepsake was so precious, although I'd heard stories. True? Not true?

I walked over to the fireplace and touched the rock. It was hard and cool, just like any ordinary rock. I lifted the case from its spot, leaving a shiny-clean rectangle bordered by dust. The box was sturdy, but most of its surprising weight must have owed to the rock itself.

My fingers brushed up against something, and I turned the frame around. Taped to its back with brittle-looking yellowed tape was an old yellowed envelope. *Matthew's* was written on it in cursive letters that I could barely read. Grandpa's writing, I decided.

"That you, Russell?" Mom called.

She looked up as I walked into the kitchen. "It could have been anybody," I said. "I thought you were gonna lock the door after I left."

"I know Port Orford—I grew up here, remember. The door doesn't need to be locked." She'd gotten thin enough in the past month to pass for a high school kid, except for the dark shadows around her eyes. She was on the worrying-about-your-dad diet, the one where you spend all day not eating much and trying to figure out what to do with all the stuff collected over seventy years of someone's life. And what to do about that life itself.

I gave her a reminder, something Dad had said when we left him behind in Santa Rosa: "'Small towns have big mysteries. And big trouble.'"

"Your dad's words. I remember them. But firefighters face life's tragedies every day so they tend to be worriers. Your grandpa's never had a problem in this house."

"Dad would want it locked."

She grinned. "Okay, okay," she said. "From now on. But I'm certain you could chase away any Port Orford bad guys."

I shook my head. I was half a head taller than her now. I'd passed her up two years earlier, almost magically, on my twelfth birthday. But no bad guys would be afraid of my skinny self.

"How was the run?" she said.

"Phoebe can *fly*." I grabbed clean glasses from the dishwasher and began stacking them on a shelf. "But I kept up." Phoebe Page, the daughter of Grandpa's caretaker, was my age—fourteen—but I could already see she was going to be a star.

Mom turned and hugged me, pressing my wet shirt to my skin. "You're getting so big," she said into my shoulder.

"Bigger than you."

"I can still take you."

I had to smile. Mom hadn't given up on the idea of experience and technique winning out over size and strength. But we hadn't had one of our legendary arm-wrestling matches for a while. "In your dreams," I said.

She leaned back and looked at me. "Why don't you jump in the shower? I made some killer cookies you can deliver to your grandpa while they're still warm."

"No chance he's moving back home?" Stupid question. The steady departure of his stuff, the simple fact that we were here, should have been answer enough. But I could hope.

"Grandpa can't be on his own, Russell," Mom said. "Becky's a nurse, and a good one, and a good person, and that's why he's living with the Pages. But even if we cared for him ourselves and kept him from wandering off or burning down the house, it would only be temporary. When summer ends, we'll have to leave Port Orford and go back to California. Then what?"

"Take Grandpa with us."

"He'd get worse. Faster. At least here he still knows

where he is. Most of the time, anyway. He's getting used to being with the Pages. He'd hate leaving Oregon. In a couple of weeks, I'll list the house with a realtor. When it sells, there will be money for his care."

Why? I wondered. If I had to come up with a top ten list of reasons to leave Port Orford, I'd have zero trouble filling it. Besides being a place where my grandpa had lost his wife and then his mind, Port Orford practically wore one of those *Kick Me* signs on its rear end. It had no movie theater, no music store, no video game arcade, no running track, no baseball park, no pizza place. The weather was good for one thing: running. The ocean water was so cold I couldn't go in past my knees without threatening future generations of Nolans. Cell-phone service was almost nonexistent unless I stood on my head on the top of a tree on the top of a mountain, which meant my California friends—or I—might as well be on the moon. Our web access was dial-up, e-mail was sketchy, the nearest radio stations played music for old folks and cowboys. And I no longer owned an iPod. Ten reasons? No sweat.

All those things were bearable in small doses. I'd always liked coming to Port Orford to visit Grandpa for a weekend or a week, especially when I was younger. But I sure wasn't happy when I found out we were going to be here for a whole summer. I complained. I argued. I whined.

I suggested (futilely) that I stay behind with Dad, who of course had to work. Mom and Dad suggested (successfully) that Mom needed my help.

I turned to head upstairs. "He might thank us for taking him."

She ignored my comment. "I remember what he was," she said. "Strong, with a mind that never stopped and legs that carried him all over this coast."

"The other Grandpa." Just a couple of years before this, when he was approaching seventy, he could still run me into the ground, he was still tutoring high school kids in math. But that was then.

After my shower I locked the front door and took off for Phoebe's, trying to get there before the temperature of the cookies matched that of the cool, foggy air pushing in from the Pacific. My legs still tingled from my run. I loved the feeling. I loved being a runner.

Had my parents known something when they decided to name me Russell Ulysses? Did they guess that the initials for those names, added to the *N* for Nolan, would turn out to be some kind of weird prediction? I figured not. I figured it was just a coincidence, especially since neither Mom nor Dad was a crystal-ball gazer, and Ulysses was an old family name.

I stretched out my stride, munching on a warm cookie,

wondering where Grandpa's dreams would take him today. Somewhere in the past, for sure. Maybe to the mountains when he was young, and ancient trees stood tall and water ran clean. Maybe to the times he sailed his first boat or went off to war or got married or became a dad.

Maybe to not so long ago, to the summer of my ninth birthday, when he and I and nobody else backpacked into a small secret beaver pond high in this coastal range. Grandpa had his own trail, but it was somewhere in his head, so he showed me how to read a compass and we bushwhacked through dense woods to get there. And when we finally did, hot and tired but wide awake at the same time, we caught trout as big as torpedoes and roasted marshmallows and waved them through the dark like torches. And later that night, when we got ready to sleep under the stars like wolves, he spread out my sleeping bag close to his and close to the fire because we'd seen fresh bear tracks. I was afraid a bear with paws the size of mud flaps and teeth like daggers would come sniffing around looking for fresh and tender boy-meat.

I loved wandering the wilderness with Grandpa back then. But I hated it when he wandered away now. These days when he took off, his destination wasn't some real-life beaver pond high in the hills. Now his journeys took him to the past, where I couldn't go—no matter how well I read a compass, how diligently I swung a machete and chopped out a trail through the thick woods.

Grandpa had pretty much checked out of the present. He could remember the long-ago as if it had happened yesterday; it was the actual yesterday—or moments ago—he couldn't recall.

I broke into a jog. Maybe I could catch him at a good moment, one of those rare times when his head bobbed to the surface of another pond—a dark mysterious pond—and he seemed to be himself again.

Chapter Three

Nice to See You:
July 20, Present

When I got to Phoebe's house, Grandpa was on the front porch, wrapped in his blanket, rocking in his high-backed rocker, gazing out toward the ocean, a short three blocks away. From where he was sitting, anyone facing west could look past a scattered collection of houses and other low buildings and watch white surf roll and crash.

"Hi, Grandpa," I said, climbing the steps, hoping for some kind of reaction. He blinked, didn't turn, resumed staring.

I waved to Phoebe, busy with something behind the open kitchen window. Dishes, I guessed, as a rainbow bubble the size of a ping-pong ball escaped through the gap. Her dark wavy hair was shower-wet and pulled back in a ponytail. She looked recovered from the run—five miles on Port Orford's streets, the beach, the highway.

She'd made it look easy. I *tried* to make it look easy.

She was tall, nearly my height. I'd heard from her proud mom that Phoebe could outrun any boy in her eighth-grade class. I wanted to believe the boast; it would make me feel better whenever (all the time, pretty much) I struggled to keep up with her.

From the window, Phoebe could watch Grandpa. If he decided to wander, she could head him off. Even in Port Orford, there were places—the highway, the cliffs, the ocean—where an old, confused person could stumble into trouble.

She pointed at her eye. According to her, this was Port Orford sign language for "Nice to see you." I had a feeling she'd made it up—the country kid trying to put one over on the city kid. But I'd gotten used to going along with it. I pointed at mine, then bent down, gave Grandpa a hug, and handed him the bag of cookies. "Chocolate chip," I said. "Your favorite, Grandpa. Warm from the oven."

"Hildie's making me a cake," Grandpa said. "She'll be here in a bit."

"Great," I said. "But have one of these in the meantime."

"Don't mind if I do," Grandpa said, and I breathed out a sigh of relief. Grandma Hildie wasn't going to appear out of the past, carrying a cake.

I pushed through the half-open front door into the cool darkness of the entryway and a cloud of breakfast smells. I heard the shower clank on upstairs, rattling the old pipes in the old house. Isaac, Phoebe's brother, was beginning his morning ritual. Lately, he came down for breakfast. When he'd first come home from the naval hospital, zombied down on painkillers and antidepressants, he rarely made it downstairs. We'd arrived in Port Orford about the same time, but for weeks I heard only rumors of the big brother home from the war, his leg mending, his spirit lagging.

By the time I finally saw him, I had this vague image in my head of what he'd look like—grim battle-worn face, buzz cut, Marine's muscles, big limp. But I couldn't have been much further off. Aside from his eyes, which seemed too old, too jumpy, his face was still a kid's. He had a nice smile and long straight hair that reached down to the collar of his T-shirt. His handshake was firm but friendly. He had muscles, but they were basketball-player muscles, long and lean. His limp was subtle. Phoebe told me that in high school he'd been a star—a six-foot-three-inch leaper, twenty points a game and unselfish.

I walked into the kitchen. Phoebe smiled an understanding smile, taking away some of the sting of Grandpa's sad condition. I'd known her less than two months, since Mom and I moved into Grandpa's place at the end of the school year, but it seemed like longer. Between me visiting Grandpa and our running, we'd spent a lot of time together. And she wasn't at all like the standoffish girls who seemed to run my school back at home. "Where's your mom?" I said.

"Getting groceries. Our new guest shows up today."

"Another Alzheimer's?"

"No," she said. "He's got other problems."

I wondered what other problems could make someone give up his independence. "You have time to hang out?"

"I don't know," she said. "Maybe later." Phoebe had to help her mom a lot. Now she plunged her hands into one side of the double sink. Laundry, not dishes, floated in the murky rinse water. She wrung out a piece of clothing and threw it into a plastic bucket. "It figures—as soon as Dad leaves, the washer goes ka-ploo-ey."

I was tempted to remind her that I was without a dad for the whole summer. Phoebe's was gone for only a couple of weeks, teaching a writing course in Iowa. "Let me help," I said instead.

"You don't—"

I'd show her how to *really* wring. I reached to pick up something, but saw what looked suspiciously like . . . women's—or girls'—underwear.

I froze.

"But thanks for offering," she said, turning pink. I felt myself doing the same. "There's not much. Mom took the big stuff to the laundromat."

We raced away from the topic of laundry to less delicate subjects—running, coaches, teachers, Grandpa, the weather, anything. From time to time, one of us would lean forward for a better look at the porch, where Grandpa continued to rock.

"Why are you guys taking people in?" I said.

Phoebe thought for a moment. "Mom says it's a chance to grow," she said. "And nursing is what she's trained to do. And there's the money, of course. Dad loves being a teacher and writer. But put both of those jobs together, and it doesn't add up to much. We'd still have a hard time getting by. They'd have a hard time paying for my college. And Mom gets to stay home with her favorite daughter."

The Page family car pulled into the driveway. "I'll help your mom," I said, heading out, eager to use that laundry-wringing energy on something less embarrassing.

"I can carry these, Mrs. Page," I said as I grabbed grocery sacks from the trunk.

"Becky," she said. "By now, it has to be *Becky*, Russell. Or I'll have to start calling you *Mr. Nolan.*"

We unloaded groceries, then Mrs. Page—*Becky*—left

the kitchen. I heard her talking to someone. I heard a man giving intelligent responses. Isaac.

Outside, a yellow taxi, a rarity in Port Orford, drove up. Becky hurried down the steps, followed by Isaac. He looked like he'd lost more of his limp since I'd seen him a few days earlier.

"Legs," Phoebe said, as we watched from the window.

"What?"

"Legs," she repeated. "The newest addition to our household."

The taxi driver opened the back door just as Becky and Isaac got to the car. The passenger—a guy—swung his legs out and struggled to his feet with Isaac's help. Legs was tall, bent at the shoulders, and thin. Probably only in his fifties, but his unruly, thick hair was nearly white.

He stood still, staring out but not at anything in particular, the way a bear stands on its hind legs and sniffs the air, until the taxi driver placed a cane in his outstretched hand. A white cane.

Legs was blind.

Chapter Four

Legs Leland:
July 20, Present

I followed Phoebe outside.

"Take this, Becky," Legs said, giving her the cane. His voice came out soft and raspy. "I ain't that blind yet, as you can see." He tottered toward the porch. Isaac shadowed him on one side, Becky on the other, as he climbed the stairs, holding his arms out at his sides like a tightrope walker. "Home from the war, Isaac?" he said when he reached the top. "Shrapnel in your flesh?"

"That's right, Legs."

"Long time since you came to see me."

"Before graduation. Before the Corps. Over a year."

"I missed ya, Isaac." He wrapped up Isaac in a long bear hug. He was a bit shorter than Isaac, but not much. "Bad times go slow."

"They do," Isaac said.

Legs nodded. "Where's that little girl?" His gaze shifted down, to Phoebe, then me, and back. "You have to help me out, youngsters. I can see there's two of you, but I don't see faces. I'm thinking one of you is Phoebe, all grown up."

"Here, Legs," Phoebe said. She began to do the point-at-her-eye thing but switched to a big hand-wave instead.

"Not 'Uncle Rocky' anymore?" Legs said.

Phoebe's puzzled look turned into a smile. "I forgot that name."

"You were a squirt," Legs said. "How about a squeeze?"

"If you promise not to fall on me." Phoebe climbed the stairs with me on her heels. She put her arms around Legs's narrow middle.

He rested his chin on her head and hung on. "You smell so good."

"Long shower. My friend Russell tried to wear me out."

"Hi, Russell," Legs said. He stuck his hand out toward me. We shook. He had a grip like an anaconda. I was relieved when he released my crushed fingers and they were able to morph back to their usual shape.

"Hi . . ." I said. Was I supposed to call this guy *Legs?*

He kept his gaze on me. Friendly, mostly, with something harder around the edges. "Kate Nolan's Russell?"

"You know my mom?"

"Your mom's a peach, son. Count your blessings."

Grandpa rose from his chair. "Smells like a mountain man," he said. His eyes flashed in a way I barely recognized. I thought about flaming marshmallows in the night, his face across the campfire.

"Art?" Legs said, turning from Phoebe, staring open-mouthed in Grandpa's direction. "Art Bellows?"

"What did they do to your eyes, Legs?" Grandpa took Legs by the hand and they shook, not letting go, as if both of them were afraid of what might happen if they did.

"Nothin'," Legs said. "It was the sugar diabetes that ruined my eyes. But I'm gonna get 'em fixed now."

"Good." It was amazing—Grandpa was tuned in. How could *I* make that happen?

"You're staying here, now, Art?" Legs said. "Becky didn't tell me."

"Just until Hildie comes for me." Not tuned in.

"What?" Legs bent forward and peered into Grandpa's face. Legs's own face seemed to collapse, suddenly aging ten years.

"Hildie," Grandpa said. "She'll be tickled to see you."

Legs cleared his throat. He let go of Grandpa's hand and patted him on the shoulder. "Uh-huh," he said finally.

"Uh-huh." He aimed a half-shocked, half-questioning look at Becky, then Isaac, then me. Like we could give him an answer.

"Nice seeing you, Legs," Grandpa said, and shuffled back to his chair with Legs staring after him.

"Who is he?" I whispered to Phoebe once Legs had made his way down to the far end of the porch, Becky and Isaac staying close.

"Louis Leland," Phoebe said. "Our old next-door neighbor. Our friend."

"You call him *Legs?*"

"*Everyone* calls him Legs. He was a surveyor for the Forest Service. He spent twenty-five years walking the mountains."

"Where's he been?"

The taxi pulled away, kicking up gravel. Legs cocked his head at the sound, face to the ocean. He breathed in like a hungry man gulping down a steak dinner.

"Prison," Phoebe whispered.

Chapter Five
Matthew: July 20, 1856

U p close, the mountain didn't look as bald. No proper trees grew from its upper half, but still it was dappled with green wherever the seeds of grasses and ground cover had managed to find a patch of dirt.

It had taken longer to get here than Matthew had estimated, but considering the difficulty of the terrain, the ups and downs of the mules' temperament, he'd not been far off. They'd reached the mountain's base, and plenty of light still coated the shoulders of the hills. The angle of the sun and the grumblings of his stomach told him it must be near suppertime.

The doctor had supplied no answers to the questions he'd raised that morning. Every so often, he stopped to take a sample of plant or dirt or rock, or have Lemieux or Poirier climb or fetch or dig to add something to his bags and boxes of specimens, and then the party would be off again. The doctor talked mostly to himself, the Canadians talked mostly to each other, and Matthew talked mostly to the mules. They responded with annoyed snorts and bared teeth and soft, musical brays meant to tell him of overwork and undernourishment.

The party stopped for the evening in a creekside clearing. Dr. Evans told Poirier and Lemieux to set up camp while he went off on his own. Matthew knew the routine well. He tethered the mules to trees, unloaded the packs from their backs, fed and watered them, and brought water to the campsite. Lemieux was the cook, Poirier his assistant. They never asked Matthew for his preferences, but he'd found the food good and plentiful. Tonight the main course was trout; in the creek Poirier had trapped two, rainbow-sided, nearly as long as Matthew's arm. They lay near the fire in a basket woven of green branches, waiting for the flames to dwindle to red heat.

The doctor returned at near-dark. Matthew expected him to be stooped from the day's efforts, but he strode tall into camp, went straight to one of the mule packs, and foraged through it. When he finally came to the fire and stretched out, he had a handful of tools—a hammer, several chisels. He rolled the chisels back and forth across his palm. A few feet away, Matthew sat on fir boughs and watched the bright metal and the doctor's dancing eyes glint in the firelight.

Sleep wouldn't come easily to Dr. Evans. Matthew knew it, but he didn't know why. Did it have to do with the secret of this mountain?

Lemieux threaded three stout green limbs through the fish basket, fashioning a triple spit, then suspended the basket between two flat-topped rocks on opposite sides of the flickering coals. In moments the fire started to hiss and snap as fat dripped from the roasting fish. Matthew's mouth watered at the smell.

"Young stomachs shouldn't have to wait so long for their sustenance," the doctor said. "The next time I'll be arriving this late, I'll tell the cook to start without me."

"I don't mind," Matthew said. "My stomach has felt hunger before. And sometimes anticipation is best."

"Insightful, young Matthew. But, oh, anticipation can be so hard."

Dr. Evans was staring into the fire, but Matthew had a feeling the doctor wasn't anticipating his next meal, no matter how good it smelled.

The doctor stopped toying with the tools and laid them in his lap. His face, dark on one side, brightened by firelight on the other, looked like the half moon rising over the mountains.

Matthew nodded at the tools. "Did you find something?"

Instead of answering, Dr. Evans looked up at the moon. When he finally spoke, his voice was church-service low. "Have you ever touched a piece of the sky?"

"Only in my dreams."

"Tomorrow, at daybreak, you and I will take a journey to the stars."

Chapter Six

Things in the Hills:
July 20, Present

Just as I was about to launch a boatload of questions, Becky and Isaac herded Phoebe into the house with them, leaving me and my curiosity stewing on the porch. Grandpa kept rocking, back in his world again. Legs steadied himself against the thick corner pillar, facing the house next door.

"What do you see?" Phoebe asked him when she returned a little while later.

"Shapes and shadows," Legs said. "Light and dark. But I'm going to a real doctor soon. I'll be good as new."

"That's great," she said in her cheerful voice, the fake one she used when there was no reason to be cheerful. This was one of only two irritating things I'd discovered in her. I hoped to keep *my* many faults undetected.

Legs kept staring out. "The people that bought my

27

house. Are they there now?" He began pacing.

"The Fords?" Phoebe said. "No—they don't come much. This is a vacation house for them. Their friends the Warrens—the people who built the new house behind your old place—aren't there, either."

"Sometime people," Legs muttered. "I wish they weren't there at all."

Phoebe gave my arm a tug, and I followed her down the steps. "What's with Legs?" I asked.

"I don't know. He seems nervous."

"I mean what's his story?"

She looked up at Legs, who was still pacing. "Come on." We moved to the far corner of the yard.

"Legs was in the state prison at Salem. He served seven years—manslaughter. He got out early for good behavior and because his health is so bad."

"Manslaughter?" I said. "He *killed* someone?"

Phoebe put her finger to her lips. "Trying to defend himself against a guy called Mace Mullins."

"What happened?"

"An argument. A scuffle. I don't know exactly."

Legs's harmless-old-guy image faded. I'd never been around someone who'd killed someone else, even in self-defense. Or had I? What about Isaac? "What started it?"

Phoebe frowned. "Legs wouldn't say, exactly.

A business venture. A prospecting operation."

"Gold?"

"I don't think there's gold around here. Other stuff, though. I've heard rumors of things in the hills. Legs was always bringing rocks home. You should ask him."

Things in the hills? What could they be? I wondered.

A few minutes later we returned to the porch, where Grandpa continued to rock and Legs continued to pace and gaze out.

"Planning on going somewhere, Legs?" Phoebe said.

Slowly, deliberately, he leaned over the far railing and angled his face east, toward the mountains. "You never know, little girl," he said. "You never know."

Phoebe raised her eyebrows at me, like *Whatever*. We both knew Legs couldn't go far.

He turned back to us. "Full Moon Mullins. He comes around, you tell me."

"How would I recognize him?" asked Phoebe calmly, like she'd expected the request.

"Younger than me, taller than me, thick-bodied."

"That's a lot of guys," I said.

"Check out his right bicep. Look for a bullet-hole scar shaped like a full moon."

"What's his real name?" I said.

"His mother named him Joseph. She had the good

fortune to die before he became Full Moon."

"Is he related to Mace Mullins?" I said.

Legs tilted his head at me. "You been talking to Phoebe?"

"I told Russell about Mace," Phoebe said.

"Full Moon is Mace's brother," Legs said, his useless eyes growing cold. "Younger. Meaner." He scuffed toward the railing while I tried to imagine this creepy Full Moon Mullins dude.

"I was just talking to your grandpa," Legs said, moving from one scary topic to another. "We had a nice little memory swap."

"I guess you know Grandpa pretty well," I said, still wondering why Legs wanted us to watch for Full Moon.

"I did. We go way back. Fished together. Walked the hills together. Rock-hounded together. I learned a lot about this country from him. He remembers some of those old times. He just doesn't remember what he had for breakfast."

For a killer and ex-convict, or just as a human being, Legs seemed like an okay guy, but I didn't need him telling me how lame Grandpa's memory had gotten, how things had changed from the old days.

Grandpa's dementia. Legs's diabetes. Growing old looked more and more like a curse. I'd had enough for now. I headed home, hoping to find an e-mail from Dad.

Chapter Seven

Like Bigfoot or Something:
July 21, Present

Early the next morning, Phoebe and I ran stride for stride north through town. The conversation was confined to runners' talk: Stretched? Laces double-knotted? Want a drink? As usual, she had her cheapo music player strapped to her arm and plugged into her ears. She'd never offered to share it—her second and most glaring fault—and I wasn't about to ask. My iPod had been ripped off from my locker just before school got out. It was a painful loss, made worse by my being trapped in the music wasteland of Port Orford.

It wasn't until we reached the beach that I asked the question that had gnawed at me overnight. "What else do you know about this Full Moon?"

"Lived around here, until Mace died," Phoebe said, loud over her music. "Full Moon's the one thing my parents worried about, bringing Legs to live with us. He's been in prison, too, for armed robbery. But he's out now."

"He'd get even with a blind guy?"

"Mom doubts it. But she worries. Our police force isn't exactly big-city. I told her and Isaac what Legs said yesterday."

"Maybe Legs grew a big imagination during all those years in jail," I said. "Maybe he's exaggerating, building up Full Moon into something he's not."

"Full Moon's *real*," Phoebe said.

We ran north on the beach until a steep rock outcropping met the water and turned us around. Fog hung above the sand. Phoebe stayed with me, putting on her competitive look. Wind and mist and her momentum had plastered small strands of hair against her forehead; her ponytail dipped and flowed behind her like the tufts of tall grass that bordered the high tide mark.

We ran out of beach and circled back to the access road. At the highway we turned north for ten minutes, then doubled back. Logging trucks—some empty, some piled high—blasted past, raising whirlwinds of debris. I held my breath, then resumed my pattern: quick exhale on one step, slow inhale on the next three. After four years of distance running, it was automatic.

We got back to Phoebe's house. She went inside to get us something to drink, taking her music with her, of course, while I stayed out front, cooling down, stretching against a gnarled apple tree. The porch was empty.

I heard a door close. Curious, I peeked around the tree into the side yard. I was surprised to see Legs, tottering away from the shed, pausing every few feet to get his bearings. As he got close to the house, he stopped and wiped his hands on the dewy grass and his baggy pants, muddy at the knees. Muttering under his breath, he wobbled into the front yard and up the porch stairs. He settled into one of the rockers as if he'd been there the whole time.

I waited a few moments and climbed the steps, noisy on purpose, breathing hard and landing heavily, dying to ask Legs what he'd been doing. Instead I asked, "My grandpa inside?"

"I believe he is, Russell," Legs said. His fingernails were rimmed with dirt.

"You having a good morning?"

"I've had better." He looked lost and miserable. His tougher side was nowhere in sight.

"Can I help?"

"Fix my eyes for me," he said as Phoebe came out with a pitcher of something red and three glasses of ice on a tray.

"He's going to the doctor soon," she said in her fake-cheerful voice. But she frowned when I pointed out Legs's fingers.

"Tomorrow," Legs said. "A real doctor, not some prison quack."

"I brought you a glass, Legs," Phoebe said. "Want some fruit punch?"

"Sounds good, Phoebe," he said. "But all that sugar would kill me."

"No sugar," she said. "Chemicals only."

"Slower death," Legs said. "Don't mind if I do."

Legs held a glass while Phoebe poured. The dark earth under his nails stood out against his pale prison skin. I motioned for her to follow me down the steps.

"We'll be out in the yard," Phoebe told Legs.

I waited until we were out of earshot. "He was digging."

"Really? Where?"

"I don't know. I saw him leaving the shed."

"Let's look."

Once at the little building, we opened the door and peered inside at the contents: lawn mower, garbage can, yard tools. I picked up a short-handled shovel. Fresh dirt and grass clung to its business end. "Someone in your family been working?"

Phoebe shook her head. "Legs."

We searched the side yard, looking everywhere for signs of digging. We explored the backyard, the far side, the front, and ended up back at the shed.

I felt chilled. I needed a hot shower, but I wasn't ready to leave.

"Maybe we should just ask him," I said.

Phoebe turned to the house next door. "His old place. Maybe he was digging *there*," she said, starting off.

I hurried to catch her. We made a quick sweep around Legs's old house and yard, front to rear.

At the back boundary stood a cedar fence, barely weathered. Beyond it was the Warrens' house, tall and white and empty. "Look," Phoebe said, fingering the grass at the base of the fence. She peeled back a rectangle of loose turf. Below the section of lawn the soil was freshly turned. Small clumps of dirt lay on the surrounding grass.

I sank the shovel deep, hoping for—what? Stolen loot? Maybe Legs had gotten to know some thieves. Maybe he'd let one of them bury something here. I stabbed with the shovel again. Nothing.

I replaced the piece of grass and prodded the ground at a suspicious-looking spot a foot up the fence line to our right. The turf lifted, and Phoebe pulled it back. Nothing, again. We continued on, locating more digging spots but nothing else.

"Now what?" Phoebe said as I closed the shed door. We started for the front yard.

"Keep an eye on him. Maybe he'll try again."

"I'm supposed to not let Legs out of my sight and worry about your grandpa, too? And what about Full Moon?"

"I'll help you," I said. "Legs is *blind*. And this Full Moon stuff sounds like an exaggeration, or some kind of legend." I was still hoping.

"I told you, Full Moon's real. He's not a legend. Port Orford legends come out of the hills."

"Like Bigfoot or something?" I made myself tiptoes-tall and stiff-legged and shuffled toward her with my arms outstretched.

She laughed. "For sure. But the legends I remember were about a giant meteorite. I think Legs used to talk about it. I heard the librarian talking about it once. It's out there somewhere, they say."

The librarian. I'd spent a chunk of time at the library since we'd arrived in Port Orford. The librarian there, Mrs. Lessing, had a sense of humor, and she was good at telling stories to the little kids who showed up on Saturday mornings. Was the meteorite legend just another story?

And then there was that special rock on Grandpa's mantel. It was supposed to be a chunk of meteorite. Grandpa had gotten it from his father, who'd gotten it from his father, who'd . . . I'd lost track. I hadn't believed the tale long enough to worry about which ancestor gave whatever to some other ancestor. And it wasn't as if it was a chunk of gold or something valuable.

But what if Grandpa's rock was connected to Phoebe's meteorite legend? Unless Port Orford was some kind of meteorite magnet, how many meteorites could there be in these hills, anyway? "My grandpa's got a rock he says is from a meteorite."

"From around here?"

I shrugged. That was another detail I hadn't worried about.

"If it is, maybe the meteorite story's true." She touched my forehead, where sweat had dried to salty grit. "You better go home and get in the shower. It's chilly. This isn't California."

I nodded, but I was thinking of something else. I was thinking of asking Grandpa about the meteorite. What if it—the story, anyway—could be our connection? What if the combination of the meteorite and his old pal Legs and his favorite (and only) grandson—me—would be the right one to open the lock on Grandpa's world?

Chapter Eight

Fences:
July 21-22, Present

I got a call from Phoebe that night. A parole officer had shown up late in the afternoon, asking questions, setting down rules about Legs reporting in, people he could see, places he could go, things he could do. Legs still seemed fidgety, Phoebe said, but even though there were no restrictions on him roaming the neighborhood, he hadn't left the house again.

I started the next day by carrying a zillion boxes of Grandpa's stuff up from the basement. After Mom and I sorted it into more boxes and bags and garbage sacks, I moved most of it again, this time to the garage.

Grandpa's rock stayed on the mantel. I got it down again as Mom walked into the living room. "What do you know about this?" I asked her.

"Your grandpa's heirloom. From a meteorite, supposedly. Handed down through the generations."

"The meteorite that people around here talk about?"

"The Port Orford meteorite. The legendary one," Mom said.

"Matthew's," I said, turning the shadow box around so Mom could see the writing.

"Your great-great-great-grandfather, Matthew Bellows. Ulysses's dad. He's the one who found it. Supposedly."

"What's in the envelope?"

"I don't know. It's been sealed and taped up as long as I can remember."

"You weren't tempted to look?"

She fingered the old tape. "Often. But Grandpa would've known."

Not now he wouldn't, I wanted to say. Not when he doesn't even know who I am.

But Mom would know. If I got into the envelope, Mom would know. I set the rock back on the mantel. "Maybe Grandpa will tell me," I said.

Mom smiled a half-sad smile. "You should ask him."

I went for an easy three-miler, hurried through an extra-hot shower, grabbed a quick sandwich, and headed to Phoebe's.

When I walked into the dining room, Grandpa and Legs were finishing up their lunch. Becky set a bowl of cherries on the table in front of Legs. She frowned as he felt for the bowl and took a handful. Some fingernail dirt remained. "Out looking for worms?" she said, taking his wrist.

Feeling a little like a junior detective, I watched Legs's face. "Just running my hands through the good soil," he said. Innocent words, but his hands dove under the table. Guilty. Of what?

"More cherries, Art?" Becky said.

"Can't eat 'em," Grandpa said. "Hives as big as footballs." But a mound of cherry pits sat on his plate. He spit another one into his hand through red-stained lips, added it to the pile, and peered up at me. Curiosity, not recognition, crossed his face. *Who is this kid?*

I had to figure out a way to talk to him about meteorites while he could still understand what I was talking about, but what chance did it have, really? If he couldn't remember he'd just eaten a pound of cherries, would he remember anything about a meteorite legend or what he'd stuck in an envelope decades ago?

I thought about the faded photo of Grandpa that sat next to the mantel rock. In it he stood unbent and looking like I'd never seen him look—suit, tie, white shirt tight at the collar, dark hair slicked down. And beside him, leaning in, arm in arm, stood his high school honey, Hildie Winters, beautiful in a long dark dress with her hair piled high on her head like a queen or something. Had my grandparents really been that young and alive and ready for whatever?

I went to the porch with Grandpa and Legs, who began their afternoon activities: sitting, staring, pacing.

By the time Phoebe joined us, Legs was peering toward his old house again. "Any moves?" she whispered.

I shook my head.

A breeze came up, driving Grandpa inside. Loud and clear, Phoebe told Legs we were heading in, and we did, but we hurried straight out the back door.

Once outside again, we sat on the back-corner lawn, where the shed was in plain view. Minutes ticked by.

Phoebe's gaze shifted. Her finger went to her lips. "Shhh."

Legs was stalking the shed. He felt his way to the door and went in. A moment later he came out holding the short-handled shovel. He walked a snaky path for the fence.

He crouched and felt through the grass, lifted the edge of a loose piece of sod, put it back, moved down a foot, tried again. When he reached an area he hadn't dug up already, he rose unsteadily and sank the shovel into the soft ground, working it around in a U-shape until he could lift a flap of turf and explore the layer of dirt underneath it. Then he moved down the fence to another untouched spot and started over.

He lifted and moved and dug and scooted on until finally he arrived at the end of the fence. He wiped his fingers through the grass and stood, leaning on the shovel. He stared at the ground along the fence, then lifted his face to the sky, as if whatever he was looking for had flown away and was up there, hiding in a dark cloud. At last he headed back to the shed.

He was through digging, and judging by the way his shoulders slumped, maybe forever. If we were going to find out what he was looking for, we'd have to come up with another way.

He disappeared around the corner of the house. The front door slammed.

"You think your mom or Isaac might have a clue?" I said.

"I don't wanna freak out Mom."

"Isaac, then."

Phoebe went inside. In a minute she was back with Isaac in tow, limping slightly, looking a little irritated. He nodded hello to me.

"You wanna take a walk with Russell and me?" Phoebe said.

Isaac shrugged, as if going on a walk with his kid sister and her little friend wasn't tops on his list of things to do. But he didn't say so.

For three blocks we moved in silence. I almost didn't want to know what was behind Legs's expeditions. What if he was doing something that would put him back in prison?

"Have you noticed Legs acting weird?" Phoebe asked Isaac. Nothing but highway and shore lay between us and the ocean now, and I couldn't take my eyes off the big waves. They came and came and bottomed out, curling into walls of white, thundering down on sand and rocks.

"Weird?" Isaac said. "You're asking *me* to tell you if someone's acting weird?"

"Yes," Phoebe said. "We need your opinion."

"I know he's a nice guy who's seen better days," Isaac said. "'Half legs and all heart,' Dad once said about him. He's acting jumpy, but what's normal for someone just out of prison?"

"Have you seen him go anywhere?" I said.

"Where would he go?"

"Next door," Phoebe said. "His old house. We saw him digging there. Twice."

"With a shovel and his bare hands," I said.

Moving at Isaac's pace—still cautious—we crossed the highway, climbed down the rocks, and arrived at the beach. The surf sound was deafening. Shore smells—seawater and decaying fish and aging seaweed and ancient logs—filled my head.

"I don't know what he'd be after," Isaac said finally. "Where was he digging?"

"Along the Fords' back fence," Phoebe said.

"Just along the fence?" Isaac said.

"Yeah," I said.

"Let's keep walking," he said. "I need the exercise." We retraced our steps back to the highway.

"Legs has told me some great stories about his younger

43

years," Isaac said. "Roaming the mountains, digging up rocks, reeling in trophy fish. He's got a better memory for names and places than I do. I don't know why he can't find whatever he's hunting."

"Maybe he wasn't the one who buried it," I said.

Isaac nodded. "Or maybe somebody already dug it up."

When we got back to the house, we went to the fence. Isaac examined the loose turf, then stood, grinning. "When Legs still owned this place—before the property was subdivided and sold to pay off his bills, before the Warrens' house was built—there was another fence."

"I remember it now," Phoebe said.

"They tore it down when construction on the new house started," Isaac said. "Once the house was built, a new fence went up."

"In the same place?" I said.

"Closer to Legs's house," Isaac said. "His yard was deeper before. He had the old fence back where the woods used to begin, at least fifteen feet behind this one."

"He doesn't know?" I said.

"He wasn't here when the property was divided," Phoebe said.

"He's blind," Isaac said. "It's impressive he even *found* the fence."

"We could get the shovel and look," I suggested.

"Yeah," Phoebe said.

"No," Isaac said. "It'll wait. I'm tired now. I've got to

take my meds and a nap. And we need to talk to Legs first. Tomorrow we can tell him what we figured out. You guys running in the morning?"

"Early," I said. "We'll go early, then talk to Legs."

"I haven't worked my way up to 'early' yet," Isaac said. "I've cut back on the pills, but they still fog me out. Is ten okay?"

"We'll be ready," Phoebe said.

Chapter Nine
Let's Do It!
July 23, Present

The next morning I hobbled up Phoebe's porch steps, right calf complaining. I was paying a price for not stretching or warming up or some other boring thing real runners did.

Phoebe and I had just passed the six-mile mark when I felt a deep, painful tug at my muscle. The pain got worse, then stopped getting worse, and I kept going until it turned into just a gnawing reminder that I should slow down, walk, stop. I didn't break stride, though, and Phoebe didn't notice until we were finished and I began walking.

"You pull something?" she said.

I told her what I'd done.

"Ice," she said.

"Phoebe Marie!" her mom called from the porch, where Legs sat, wrapped in a blanket like an old man. "Breakfast!"

"Marie?" I said.

She grinned. "What's yours?"

"Ulysses." I waited for a smart remark. I'd been named after Ulysses Bellows, Grandpa's grandpa, so the name wasn't exactly trendy.

"I like it," she said. "An adventurer." She watched me massage my calf. "Come with me," she said. "We have ice."

Inside, the house smelled great—roses on the entryway table, shifting to bacon as l followed Phoebe into the dining room.

Isaac looked up from his breakfast when I limped in. "Russell," he said. "You pull a muscle?"

I nodded.

"Russell the Muscle." Isaac smiled, food-cheeked. He pointed to a half-full serving plate. "Build up your strength. We'll be digging if Legs wants help."

Phoebe brought me a plastic bag filled with ice cubes. I sat, icing my leg, downing a couple pieces of bacon, watching Phoebe and Isaac eat. But I wasn't hungry. Legs could be wandering the yard, shovel in hand.

Isaac carried his dishes into the kitchen. "I'm ready to talk to him," he said when he returned.

I stood up. "Let's do it."

Suddenly Isaac stopped. His face took on a strange, vacant look.

He stood still, staring off at nothing.

"Isaac?" Phoebe said. "No!" she cried, like she'd seen this before. "No! No!"

Frozen, Isaac eyed the front door or who knew what. Something lurking behind some other door, maybe? He coiled, ready to spring.

"Isaac?" Phoebe gave me a look—*help me*—but I didn't know what to do. From the corner of my eye, I caught a flash of Becky hurrying into the room, hand pressed against her mouth.

I touched Isaac's shoulder, barely, but he jerked away and spun around. The back of his open hand flew at my face. I could only blink as the hand blurred by.

He stared at me, eyes clouded. Part of me wanted to step away, out of range of this stranger. But part of me recognized someone familiar in those eyes, a friend returning home. I stayed close. I held out my hand, palm open.

"You okay, Isaac?" Phoebe said.

Slowly the emptiness left his expression. "Sure."

"You almost hit Russell," Becky said.

"Let's do it," Isaac ordered.

"Huh?" I said.

"'Let's do it,'" Isaac repeated. "That's what Bones used to say whenever he got behind the wheel."

"Bones?" Phoebe said.

"Bonner. Our Humvee driver. Dead." Isaac shook his head.

Phoebe looked at me. "You said, 'Let's do it.'"

Isaac flinched. I remembered the words. "Sorry," I said. "I didn't know."

"Nah," Isaac said, taking my hand and shaking it, holding on tight. His grip pressed my knuckles together like the sections of a squished orange. "*I* should be sorry. I'm a loaded gun. People should get combat pay for being around me." He looked at Phoebe, who was trying on her cheerful look. "But I'm getting better, right, Phoebs?"

"You're not a loaded gun," she said.

Becky moved close and gave him a hug. "You *are* getting better."

"You didn't hit me," I said.

Isaac attempted a smile. "That's one positive."

"Let's—" I began. I'd almost repeated the cursed words. "Let's go outside."

Chapter Ten

Can You Dig It?
July 23, Present

Legs was sitting, facing his old house.

"When do you leave for the doctor?" Phoebe asked him.

"Your mom says one-thirty. It's clear up in Coos Bay."

The front door opened behind us. Becky came out with Grandpa in tow. "I'm taking Art for a ride," she announced. "Drugstore, hardware store, library. But we'll be back in plenty of time, Legs."

"I'll be here," Legs said resignedly. He tilted his head slightly at the sounds of footsteps on the stairs, car doors slamming, the engine starting.

"We saw you in your old yard yesterday," I began. "Looking for something."

Legs's face didn't give anything away. Prison must have taught him one thing: Don't let them know what you're thinking.

"We can help you," Isaac said. "No strings."

Legs was silent for a long time. "What makes you think so?" he said at last.

"What you're looking for was next to the fence?" I said.

"For the sake of continuing this interesting conversation, let's say it was."

"The old fence?" Phoebe said.

"What's that mean, 'the old fence'?" Legs said.

"The fence that was there when you owned the house came down when the new house went up," Isaac said. "You were digging next to the *new* fence. In a different place."

Legs grinned. "You don't say."

"The old fence would have been about fifteen feet behind the new one," Isaac said.

"A small detail a blind guy might miss," Legs said.

"So can we help?" I said.

Legs nodded. "This is a good time." He got up and shuffled toward the stairs.

The Warrens' house still looked empty. Isaac unlatched the gate. Phoebe and I searched the lawn for signs of the old fence while Isaac stepped off five strides from the new one.

He'd brought tools from the shed: a shovel, a rake, and a long-handled edger with a half-moon-shaped blade. Using the edger, he carved out a two-foot square and pried up the chunk of sod. "One of you wanna dig?"

I rammed the shovel into the soft dirt, half-expecting something exciting: the feel of metal against wood, an ancient chest locked against the elements and modern-day pirates. But the dirt surrendered easily, and I lifted out a shovelful and dumped it on the grass. "Any clues, Legs?"

"I think we're close," Legs answered. "The hole was centered on the old fence, which would have been about here, if I'm reading things right. The top of the box is about a foot down. Unless the bulldozers got it."

So there *was* a box. I worked faster, digging out the square to the depth of a foot or more.

"I kind of promised no questions," Isaac said, "but . . . "

Legs raised a bushy eyebrow. "Just old keepsakes."

"We could've kept them for you," Phoebe said.

Legs didn't reply. I refilled the hole. Isaac replaced the sod, then exposed another square of earth. "This may take a while," he said.

I had an idea. In the shed I found a four-foot-long metal rod, nearly an inch thick and heavy. I hauled it and a big sledgehammer out into the daylight.

Isaac, replacing another section of turf, looked up. "What you got?"

I planted one end of the rod in the grass. I tapped it with the sledge and felt it ease into the soft ground, then hammered it hard a couple of times, and it plunged deep, more than a foot. I worked it back out.

"A probe," Isaac said, fingering a few days' growth of

sparse chin whiskers. "Good thinking, Muscle."

Legs held out his hand aimlessly, but I moved the rod so he could feel it. "A genius," he said.

A *genius*. I stood a little taller and repositioned the bar.

We explored in one direction, then went back and started toward the other end of the yard.

"You want to hold this while I get it going, Legs?" I said.

Isaac placed Legs's hand on the rod. Legs held on tight. Three swings and the rod was buried deep. We pulled it back out and moved to another spot, Legs hanging on, Phoebe handling the hammer this time.

She drove the rod steadily deeper.

It stopped. Legs's eyes lit up like night windows.

Isaac handed him the shovel. On his second thrust, the blade clanked to a halt. He gave the shovel to me and knelt, working his hands into the dirt. "Get me some grasping room, Russell."

I dug, felt something solid, and worked the shovel around it, lifting out clods of dirt. I watched a shape—a dirt-encrusted rectangular lump, maybe a foot-and-a-half long and half as wide—form in the hole. "Go for it, Legs."

Legs felt around with one hand while he scraped away soil with the other. He brushed at the top of the object—a toolbox, I decided—until a handle emerged. He raised it upright and tugged while Phoebe and Isaac helped, scraping and rocking and pulling.

The box broke free. Legs lifted it out of the hole and set it on the ground. He brushed off more dirt to reveal a green metal container with a stout latch and a heavy-duty brass-and-steel lock.

"That's it?" Phoebe said, but the answer was already on Legs's face.

He nodded. "Thanks, kids." He cradled the box in one arm like his long-lost child.

"You have the key?" Isaac asked.

"I do," Legs said, getting unsteadily to his feet. "Thanks," he said again as Phoebe took his elbow. "We need to fill the hole back in."

But Isaac was already kicking dirt into the hole. I headed for the fence to get a shovelful of replacement soil from the garden. "We got it," Isaac said.

"You kids are gonna spoil me," Legs said. "Wasn't anybody spoiling me where I came from."

"That's why you don't wanna go back," Phoebe said. She herded Legs toward the gate while I deposited a load of dirt, thinking about what she'd said.

Could the mysterious contents of the box get Legs in more trouble?

Chapter Eleven
Parole Officer:
July 24, Present

Early the next day I was on my way to Phoebe's, wondering how Legs's visit to the doctor had gone. My calf barely felt tight as I stretched out my stride, testing. Two blocks from the Pages', a big, dirty-brown car eased up next to me. I figured tourist, someone needing directions. I stopped; the car stopped. The passenger-side window hummed down.

Behind the wheel sat a guy wearing a white shirt and striped tie. The tie was loose, the collar was unbuttoned, the sleeves were halfway rolled up, the front of the shirt was rumpled. He leaned toward me. The face that came out of the shadows was round and creased and featured an upturned nose and two small dark eyes. He smiled, but it didn't look right: a grinning pig wasn't something I thought I'd ever see.

"Goin' to the Page house?" The man's voice was high-pitched and breathy, as if he had to force it out of his throat. And the question didn't make sense. How did he know? Had he been watching me? I hung back from the car. The guy gave me the creeps.

"Why?"

"You know a man named Louis Leland?"

I hesitated. "Are you a friend of his?"

"Not likely. I'm his parole officer. You know him, uh, fella?"

"Russell."

"You know him, Russell?"

"Kind of."

"You ever noticed him doing anything suspicious? Leaving the house? Nosing around?"

"Do you have some kind of ID? My parents wouldn't want me talking to anyone unless I knew for sure who they were."

I expected resistance—I was just a kid. But the guy didn't hesitate. He fished a wallet out of a suit coat lying on the seat, flipped it open, and flashed it in my direction. I saw a card and badge. "Mel Hanson," the man said, snapping the wallet shut. "Now whadda you say, Russell?"

"How did you know I was going to the Pages' house?"

"It's my job to know."

He's been watching the house, I thought. "You know he's blind?"

"I know everything about Legs Leland."

"Why ask me, then?"

Mel Hanson sighed impatiently. "I can't be everywhere.

I could use another set of eyes."

Not mine, I decided. "He doesn't go *everywhere*. Mrs. Page took him to the doctor yesterday. That's about it."

"So tell me if I got everybody: besides Louis, there's an old guy, Mrs. Page, and the daughter, who's a cutie, huh, Russell?" He winked and gave me a gap-toothed grin; my stomach did a slow turn. "And who's the tall, gimpy kid with the hippie hair? He looks like somethin' the tide washed in."

The morning was cool, but I found myself heating up. "He's a war hero." And he could kick your wrinkled behind, creep.

The grin stayed. "I think you and me should have a little agreement. You keep your eyes open, your ear to the ground, and if Legs goes anywhere on the sneak, you let me know." He handed me a piece of paper. "I'm at a motel just up the road. That's my number. Ask for Mel Hanson." He leaned closer, and I inched back, avoiding those shirt-button eyes.

"He's *blind,*" I said.

"Don't matter. He'll find a way to do his dirt." He stared. "So call me. And maybe I'll put in a good word for ya with that little cutie. Okay?"

I gave him my Clint Eastwood squint. When the ocean freezes over, I thought.

"Good," Mel Hanson said, as if we were now on the same team. He put the car in gear.

I watched as he slowly drove away. He wasn't going to Phoebe's house to spy. Now he had his other set of eyes—mine.

When Phoebe opened the door, I saw Grandpa and Legs at the dining room table, contemplating the remains of their breakfast. There was no sign of Isaac; he was probably still in bed.

Grandpa's gaze shifted. "You never did tell me, Legs."

I slipped behind Grandpa's chair and laid my hands on his thin but still-muscular shoulders.

"Tell you what, Art?" Legs said.

"Remember?" Grandpa said. "A few months ago. You said you'd found something in the hills. Thanks to me, you said. Said you were going to tell me about it."

"A few months . . . " Legs said, studying Grandpa's face. "It's been more—" he began. "I kind of got tied up," he said. "But I'll tell you about it, Art. Soon." I felt Grandpa's shoulders relax. He even reached up and patted me on the arm and held on for a moment. And I was glad.

But I felt a little off-balance. What was Grandpa talking about? What had Legs told him, and when? Could this have something to do with the meteorite story? Or Legs's box?

The phone rang. "Legs!" Becky called from the kitchen. "The doctor!"

Phoebe and I sat quiet, trying to hear Legs's side of the conversation.

"Hello . . . That high? . . . I gave myself the shots like

they said . . . Yeah, we'll get the other prescription, whatever it takes to get my eyes back in shape.

"Oh." He said something to Becky. She answered him, but the words were too soft to hear.

Then Legs was back on the phone: "You're sure? . . . What about in a few months? . . . What if I had a lot of money? . . . I see . . . Research . . . You never know . . . "

His voice trailed off, and then Becky was talking "Is there someone at the university he could see, Dr. Ashe? If there's a study or something, I know he'd be a good candidate . . . I understand . . . We'll get the prescription and be back in two weeks . . . Thank you . . . " She hung up and said something to Legs. He didn't answer her.

A moment later he wobbled into the dining room. He felt his way to the hallway and down to his bedroom. His door closed with a click.

Becky joined us. "Dr. Ashe," she said, as if we didn't already know. "He says the diabetes is uncontrolled and Legs needs stronger dosages of insulin. His circulation is bad. The doctor's going to talk with some eye specialists, but there's practically no hope Legs's vision will improve—unless someone comes up with a new idea."

The room went silent. "Legs, he's an iron man," Grandpa said finally. "Legs and me are going to hike up into the hills again. We're going to search the nooks and crannies for treasures."

The image of Grandpa and Legs stubbornly stumbling

through the mountains, on the track of treasures, brought a lump to my throat. And some hope to my heart. At least Grandpa was making a connection to something outside his own world, even if that something was not much more than a fantasy. How could I be a part of that connection, too?

Phoebe tried on a brave smile. "We can't let him give up."

I found myself nodding.

"Of course not," Becky said. "He's down, but he'll bounce back."

"C'mon," Phoebe said to me.

I hugged Grandpa and followed Phoebe out the door. We headed to the beach. I told her about the parole officer. I didn't tell her about the *cutie* remarks. "He asked about Legs leaving the house," I said. "Doing sneaky stuff."

"He seemed okay when he came to see Legs the other day. You think he saw us next door yesterday? Bringing back the box?"

"I don't know. But maybe the box has something to do with what he was talking about. Maybe the police expected Legs to get out of jail and lead them to something he'd stolen."

"He wasn't in jail for stealing."

"What's the guy so interested in, then? What's in that box?"

"I don't know," Phoebe said.

Chapter Twelve
Better Than Gold:
July 24, Present

Isaac was still asleep when we got back to the house. I sat next to Grandpa on the porch while Phoebe went inside to wake up her brother. Maybe he'd have an idea about what Legs had to hide.

"You and Legs used to do a lot of exploring together, Grandpa?" I said.

Grandpa peered at me as if he was trying to pick a face out of a crowd. He looked around at the empty porch. "He was young," he said finally. A smile brightened his face. Suddenly he looked like his old self. I held my breath, afraid to break the fragile connection.

"He'd hike me into the ground," Grandpa continued. "But I knew the hills, what was in 'em. We made a good pair, rock-hounding, dreaming of the big discovery."

"Gold?"

"Better." He studied my face, as though he were trying to decide on my trustworthiness. "Matthew's treasure," he whispered. "Lost."

Matthew. My great-great-great-grandfather. The name on the envelope. The *meteorite.* "What kind of treasure?" I wanted him to say it.

Grandpa stared at me again. His eyes dulled. "I want to see the girl," he said finally. *The girl* was how Grandpa sometimes referred to Mom now.

"She was here yesterday, Grandpa. She'll be back this afternoon."

He breathed deep, as if the heavy, salty air contained some magic that would repair all the short circuits in his brain.

The door opened and Legs pushed through. He felt his way to an empty chair next to me. He sat down, banging his knee on the way, cursing to himself.

"Scientists are making discoveries all the time," I told him. "Before long doctors will know a lot more about diabetes."

"Maybe," Legs said. "But I was hoping for now instead of later. For years I've been nurturing a dream, waiting to see it come true."

This was my opening. "What is it—your dream?"

When Legs finally spoke, it wasn't an answer, exactly. He looked up, past the edge of the porch roof, toward a patch of blue in the ceiling of puffy white. "You ever touched a piece of the sky?"

Grandpa was suddenly on the edge of his chair.

"A few summers ago Grandpa and I climbed this mountain called Black Butte over in central Oregon," I said. I looked at Grandpa. He was paying attention. He *was*. "We got to the top and we were hot and sweaty, but we could see a hundred miles in every direction. We sat on the highest rock and drank pop and ate lunch. We talked about staying up there, up in the sky. Forever."

"I've hiked Black Butte," Legs said, placing his big hand over Grandpa's forearm. "Sharp-edged mountains. Red, honeycombed rocks. Blue wildflowers the color of Phoebe's eyes."

I imagined Legs—younger, stronger, clear-eyed, unbent by poor health and prison—leading the way up the Black Butte trail. But the conversation had wandered away from his answer-that-was-a-question. He was being vague and mysterious and cautious, but he was trying to give me a clue. And suddenly a piece-of-the-sky/legendary-meteorite linkup happened in my head. "Grandpa thinks he has a piece of meteorite," I said. "I've touched it."

"You have?" Legs said. A grin crept across his face.

"Is that what you meant?" I said. "Touching something from space, I mean? Something that *falls* from the sky? A meteorite?"

His grin spread wider—then it vanished. "Your grandpa. Did his memory go quick?"

The change of subject caught me off guard. "Kind of," I said under my breath. "But we weren't around him much.

No one noticed right away. Or maybe no one wanted to notice. Once we did, the three of us started watching him. We were all hoping it was nothing."

Legs looked in Grandpa's direction. "Sad," Legs said. "You lose your memory, you lose your sense of who you are. It must feel like drowning."

Or prison, I decided. Where you don't trust anyone—or give straight answers.

The front door opened. "Russell?" Phoebe said. "Isaac's up."

Inside, Isaac was slouched over the dining room table, drinking coffee. Phoebe and I sat down and watched him take a long sip, the steaming cup quivering in his trembling fingers. Finally he must have decided we weren't going away. "What are you two cooking up?"

I recounted my conversation with Legs. I gave them my new theory—that whatever was in the mysterious box had something to do with the meteorite. I told Isaac about the parole officer, what he'd asked me to do.

Isaac gave a short hiss of disgust. "It isn't right."

"Should we tell Legs?" Phoebe said.

"He's already met with the parole dude," Isaac said. "He already feels like a monkey on a string. How's he gonna feel if we tell him the guy's recruiting spies?"

"What about the box?" I said. "You think he's after it?"

"What do we do?" Phoebe said.

"Don't tell Legs yet," Isaac said. "It sounds like he's opening up a bit, dropping hints. Maybe he'll come out and tell us exactly what's in the box. If it really is just old keepsakes, there's no point in worrying him. If it's something else, then we'll have to warn him. And watch for trouble."

The front door opened. Cool air pushed in, followed by Legs, on an unsteady but determined course for the hallway. He looked drained, running on empty. A moment later, his bedroom door slammed behind him.

Phoebe broke the silence. "We're not gonna see him for a while. He's probably pretty upset about his eyes."

I decided she was right. And Mom had asked for my help with Grandpa's yard. I headed for home.

Chapter Thirteen
Full Moon Mullins:
July 25, Present

The next morning I got up early, victim of a restless brain, and found Mom already kneeling on the floor of Grandpa's study, boxing up books, looking through photos. She wiped her eyes, and I looked away. We'd talked the night before about her having to do this, that Grandpa wouldn't be reading these books again, that he no longer recognized the people in the photos.

The bookcases lining the walls were nearly empty. "He asked about you yesterday," I said. "'The girl,' he calls you."

"I know." Mom laughed bitterly and brushed at her eyes again. "Two years ago he knew the names of everyone in this town. Now he thinks his own daughter is some near-stranger. But I'm planning on being there this afternoon, as usual. And I'm going to invite everyone at Becky's for lunch soon."

"At least he calls you something. Me, I'm just another ghost."

"He loves having you visit, even if he can't show it."

"I'm not with him that much, Mom. I mostly talk to the Pages and Legs."

"I hope you do. It's hard being up here, away from your friends."

"It's not that bad." Now that there was something interesting (but scary) going on, summer was turning out better than I'd expected. Maybe I'd fill out that top ten list yet. I remembered what Dad said about small towns having big mysteries. And big trouble. "Were Legs and Grandpa good buddies?"

"I remember them hiking together, rock-hounding," Mom said. "Half the rocks in your grandpa's garage were dug up on trips they made together. I wouldn't say they were close, though. Legs is probably twenty years younger than your grandpa."

"Were they in on any deals together?" I asked. "Business or something?"

Mom leaned back. "The only business your grandpa had time for was the store. Legs had his own business partner, apparently. Unfortunately."

"No one knows what Legs's business was?"

"Nothing specific came out during his trial, or before," she said. "The only thing Legs admitted to was working with Mace Mullins while they were both with the Forest Service, which was common knowledge anyway. But there were rumors that they were hunting treasure or had maybe even found something and were trying to stake a claim." She studied my face. "Why so curious?"

"I keep thinking that if I could talk to Grandpa about what's deep inside his head—interesting things like exploring the mountains with Legs, finding cool rocks, fishing, the trouble between Mace Mullins and Legs, the meteorite story—he might come back to us a little," I said. "And Phoebe and Isaac are trying to help Legs, you know, adjust. So I'm trying to help them, too."

"It's been a long time since I've lived in Port Orford," Mom said. "I wasn't here when Mace died. What I learned came from your grandpa and old friends and newspapers they sent us. I wish I could tell you more. I think it's wonderful that you're trying to help your grandpa."

"Can we open the envelope?" I said. "Maybe whatever's in there would mean something to him."

"Matthew's?"

I nodded.

She sighed. She got to her feet. "Why not?"

In the living room, I held the shadow box while Mom slipped her fingers under the envelope. The tape pulled away easily from the paper backing on the box; the glue had dried up long ago.

I carefully scissored off a sliver of one end of the envelope and pulled out a single sheet of ancient wrinkled paper, folded in thirds.

It was a map, kind of, neatly handwritten in ink. At the

top it said "north," at the bottom, "south." To the west was the Pacific Ocean and Port Orford harbor, clearly labeled. Slightly to the north of the harbor was a line snaking across the paper and designated "river." To the east were several teepee-shaped markings and the word "mountains." Among them was one that wasn't teepee-shaped; it was round-topped and bigger. Halfway up that mountain, the mapmaker had drawn an object—a circle or sphere. Under it, in capital letters, was one word:

"SOMEWHERE?"

At the bottom of the paper, in old-fashioned handwriting, was an explanation: "This is all my scarred memory can recall," a name, "M. Bellows," and a date, "September 21, 1879."

In truth, it was the lamest map I'd ever seen. What good would it do to show it to Grandpa? "This is a big help," I said. *"Somewhere?"*

"Matthew wasn't much of a mapmaker, I guess," Mom said.

Disappointed, I got fresh tape and refastened the envelope to the back of Grandpa's frame, then helped Mom box up the last of the books. Our voices echoed in the empty room.

It was nearly noon when I left for Phoebe's. Three blocks away, I heard the growl of an engine, the squeal of tires. A familiar brown car nosed out from the next cross street and headed my way. By the time it got to me, it was creeping along, half on the shoulder.

The car stopped. I looked past the glare of the windshield and saw what I'd expected to see: my buddy, the parole officer.

The passenger-side window slid down. Mel Hanson leaned toward me. He was tieless, coatless. His short-sleeved white shirt was rumpled everywhere but where it stretched across his chest. One thick forearm, blue with the ghost of an ancient elbow-to-wrist tattoo, was draped across the back of the passenger seat. "Anything to whisper to me, Russell?" he wheezed.

"I hardly see him," I said. "We barely say hello."

"You was gonna keep an eye on things for me." Mel Hanson leaned closer, grinning, but his little eyes were muddy with menace.

"He still has diabetes," I said. "He's still blind. It's pretty easy keeping an eye on him."

"You have a smart mouth, mommy's little boy," Mel Hanson said. "You need to have more respect for your elders, especially officers of the law."

"I just don't have anything to tell you."

"You think Legs Leland is some kind of hero. He's not. He's a killer with a secret. And blind or not, he's gonna find a way to wander." He leaned even closer, and for an awful moment I thought he was getting ready to leap out and grab me. His hand eased over the near edge of the seat back, his sleeve rode up.

High enough.

On Mel Hanson's bicep was another tattoo, but this one looked new. It was red, white, and blue in circular bands, like a target. Its center—the bull's eye—was red and shiny and indented.

It was a scar. Like a crater. On the moon.

I stepped back. A big guy with a scar on his right bicep, bullet-hole-sized. This guy—this parole officer, Mel Hanson—wasn't a parole officer and he wasn't Mel Hanson. This guy was Full Moon Mullins.

Why hadn't I figured it out earlier? I tore my eyes away from the tattoo, faked a yawn, stared at the gravel at my feet. "I'll keep my eyes open." Anything to make him go away.

But the big face in the window was suddenly looking at me differently. Suspiciously. Full Moon's eyes narrowed. "You got something to tell me now?"

"No."

"You sure?"

"Yes," I said, but my voice broke. I was positive he was going to see right through my lie.

"You got my phone number?"

"Yes." If *got* meant stuck to the bottom of a garbage can.

"Use it." There was a threat in his voice. "Okay?"

"Okay."

"See ya around, Russell." As he stepped on the gas,

I caught one last glimpse of the scar.

I waited for the car to turn the next corner. When it did, I set off for Phoebe's, wanting to run but afraid Full Moon would come back. So I walked, long-strided and quick. Who should I tell? Phoebe and Isaac, for sure. What about Legs? Becky? Mom? The police?

I could still see the look in Full Moon's eyes. What was he after? Revenge? The contents of Legs's box? Something else altogether? *How much danger was Legs in?*

When I got within sight of Phoebe's house, I spotted her and Isaac, standing next to a silver four-door sedan. They looked up as I crossed the street. "I gotta talk to you," I blurted out, but Phoebe put her finger to her lips and Isaac steered me back across the street, away from the house and toward the beach.

"Why the secrecy?" I said.

"Tom Betters is at the house," Phoebe said.

"Who?"

"The parole officer," Isaac said. "You didn't recognize his car?"

"A real parole officer?" I said.

Isaac and Phoebe gave me identical looks—puzzled with a capital *P.* So l told them the scar story. We compared parole officer names—Mel Hanson versus Tom Betters—and looks—big and pig-faced versus tall, thin, and bushy-haired—and came to the same scary conclusion.

Phoebe shook her head. "I should've guessed."

"How?" I said. "*I* saw him. I didn't tell you his name or what he looked like. I should've figured it out. But I guess part of me didn't believe in Full Moon."

"No harm," Isaac said. "We know who he is now, but he doesn't know we know."

"Do you think Full Moon is after whatever was in Legs's box?" Phoebe said.

"He's here for a reason," Isaac said. "Besides revenge, I mean. Full Moon thinks Legs has something valuable, and he wants it."

"He said Legs is a killer with a secret," I said.

"We need to tell Legs," Phoebe said.

"Now," Isaac said.

Chapter Fourteen
Matthew: July 21, 1856

The weather had grown dreary overnight. Sunup announced itself through a thick layer of dark clouds, and a fine drizzle fell as Matthew rolled out from under his wet blankets. Dr. Evans was up and dressed, poking at the fire.

"I was about to rouse you," he said. "It's light enough for us to make our way now. I've told Lemieux and Poirier to stay with the mules."

Matthew looked toward the lean-to of fir boughs where the Canadians had spent the night. They were still there, no doubt drier than Matthew and glad for the extra sleep. But he was happy to be up, eager to go. He remembered the doctor's words from last night: a journey to the stars.

They headed out of camp on the game trail the doctor had taken the day before. He had a small pack with his tools inside, clanking as he walked. Matthew followed close, carrying a flask of stream water and a tin of fish left over from the evening meal. He'd eaten some dried venison, some johnnycake smeared with apple butter, but his stomach still rumbled.

The drizzle fell harder as they traversed the base of the mountain, then diminished as they reached the leeward side. Now the wet came mostly from the trees towering overhead—heavy drops ticking against the brim of Matthew's hat. He hunched his shoulders and pulled his hat lower as the trail veered up.

They moved out of the forest and into an immense circular clearing. The rest of the mountain had begun recovering from whatever force of nature had swept over it, but this wasteland of dirt and patchy grass and splinters of tree and rock looked as if a giant fist had pummeled it only the day before.

The going was slick; Matthew had to watch where he placed his feet. Loose stones were scattered everywhere on the steep slope. He didn't relish the thought of a tumble down the mountain.

Dr. Evans stopped, breathing deep. "What are your thoughts, Matthew, now that you have seen this devastation?"

Thoughts. Matthew had thoughts but they were muddled. "Confusion," he said.

The doctor smiled and looked at the overcast sky. "You were very close when you chose fire as the culprit. You just needed to take it one step further."

"You mean what caused the fire."

"Exactly. I considered the humdrum causes—man, lightning—but they didn't ring true. Something about the nature of this burn—even from a distance—told me it was different."

"You saw something?"

"More properly, I *didn't* see something. Much of the mountain, above a certain level, is relatively bald, but this side—this portion of this side—is nearly barren. Dead trees stand throughout the rest of the burned area. They're black and gray and devoid of leaf and needle, but they're standing. Here . . . "

Matthew looked. The only recognizable trees lay on the ground, charred through. Circling the clearing were tree skeletons, standing like the pickets of a fence. But none stood in the clearing itself. It appeared that whatever had taken the trees down and then roasted them had blasted out from the center of the circle. He stepped on a blackened branch and watched it crumble to wet ashes beneath his boot. "Everything's blown over," he said.

"That was my thinking. So I had to ask myself what force could uproot these trees and scorch them to cinders and practically sterilize the ground below them."

Matthew couldn't think of anything reasonable. "Not lightning?"

"It would have been a bolt of lightning such as the earth has never seen before or since. As I said, I considered the possibility and then proceeded to something more likely, something you may not be aware of."

The doctor took a swig of water from his silver leather-bound flask, shouldered his pack, and moved on, making his own trail through the thick deposits of debris. "We'll be there soon," he said. "You'll see for yourself."

They moved like phantoms from one patch of fog to the next. The going was hard, but Matthew's heart thumped as much from anticipation as effort. The drizzle had stopped, and now there were no downed trees, just ashes and rock and dirt and a few low-growing, feeble plants poking through. No birds, no songs. The smell of charcoal rose thick from the doctor's footsteps. Was this what he meant by a journey to the stars? Was this barren landscape what it was like on one of those far-off twinklers?

They switched back along the mountain's face, bearing for a rock outcropping a hundred yards above them. Gradually, the outcropping took on familiar features: a nose, broken, with an eye socket on its right side.

Inside the eye socket was an eyeball.

They crossed below the nose, ascended to the eyeball, and stopped. Matthew stared. Up close, the rock—the eyeball was a rock, to be sure—looked even more eye-like. It was a different color, a different material, from all the rock and debris surrounding it. The difference was obvious, even though the rock was covered with a thin layer of dirt and ash. It had the look of a round loaf of bread fresh from the oven, its crust pocked and darkened and burnished by heat, then dusted with powder. It was nearly buried, but three or four feet of it remained aboveground, and it looked to be twice that measure across. Matthew stood back, not willing to touch it.

"What is it?"

"A piece of the sky, young Matthew." The doctor laid his pack on the ground and groped through it, bringing out hammer and chisels. A small area of the rock had been scraped clean of dirt. The doctor's work from the day before, Matthew decided.

"This is a piece of the sky?"

"A meteorite, to be precise. But it was perhaps once a piece of something much bigger, something deep in the skies. A meteorite is an extraordinary—and in this case extraordinarily large—rock that has fallen to Earth from space. This one traveled millions of miles to get here."

Millions. Matthew had a hard time with the number. He tried to picture something traveling that far. What unimaginable wonders had it passed on that long, lonely trip? "And its journey ended here," he said. "How long ago, do you think?"

"From the lack of new growth in the immediate area, the depth of the sediment in the impact cavity, the amount of grit covering the meteorite itself, I would estimate something less than thirty years," Dr. Evans said.

Thirty years. These hills were even more unsettled then, home to few but Indians and their prey. Had a party of hunters seen this huge rock fall from the sky? What would they have seen, exactly? "What do you think it looked like when it landed?"

"I've read accounts of the landings. Even stones as small as your fist are like a dozen shooting stars in one as they enter the atmosphere. A meteorite this size would come to earth like a chariot of fire. It would turn the night into day. I hope to God that someday I will see one like it."

Matthew drew closer to the rock. Dr. Evans smiled. "Do you have any idea what a meteorite this large would weigh, Matt?"

"More than the most gluttonous mule."

"Indeed. More than many mules. I expect we're only seeing a third of the whole object. I estimate the weight at more than ten tons."

Matthew whistled. "You'll take it out somehow?"

"Not now, certainly. I want to secure some samples, submit them to experts for verification, and then return here with sufficient equipment, manpower, and mule power to transport it out in pieces. A meteorite like this is worth a fortune, scientifically and monetarily."

"Will you be able to find it again?"

"I've found it twice now, but I'll make a map. Perhaps I'll bring you and your young memory back with me."

"I would like that."

"Done, then. But first things first." The doctor crouched, examining the rock, running his hand over its surface. "Help me," he said. "I'm looking for a small protuberance, something that I can split off in less than a lifetime. This meteorite is composed of extremely hard minerals."

On the opposite side Matthew began looking for an irregularity. He fingered the surface, surprised at its cool smoothness. Slowly he slid his hand down to ground level, then up, then down, feeling for knobs or indentations masked by the dirt.

He'd been at it for several minutes when his fingers bumped against a ridge of rock down low. He scraped away dirt. The ridge was two or three inches long and an inch or so wide. It was raised nearly an inch above the area around it. "I found something."

"Good lad. I believe I have, too. But let's look at yours first." The doctor knelt next to Matthew and examined the small crest. "A little difficult to reach, but exactly what I wanted." He placed a chisel blade against the wrinkle of rock. "Now let's see if we can get ourselves a sample of this specimen."

He put hammer to chisel, lightly at first, then harder, moving along one side of the bump, then the other. The hammer hit off-center and slipped, hitting his hand, and he cursed under his breath. "Stubborn," he said.

He took three more unproductive swings. "Perhaps you could find us another likely knob, Matthew," he said.

"A smaller one, more defined. The one I found is on the other side. I scraped off the surface dirt, so you should be able to see it." He went back to his pounding and Matthew began searching again.

He'd just discovered another bump, smaller and nearly bell-shaped and fully under the top inch of sediment, when he heard a loud clang. He expected more curse words. "Aha!" the doctor shouted. He sprang to his feet, holding something high. The piece of meteorite. He showed it to Matthew as he cleaned it off in a pool of rainwater.

It was the size of a rabbit's foot, dark, and shiny-wet. It didn't look much different from other rocks Matthew had seen. "Can you tell it's a meteorite for certain?"

"Not just a meteorite, lad. If I'm not mistaken, this is a pallasite meteorite—stony-iron, they're called—the rarest, most valuable of all."

Now that it was rinsed off, now that he could see the newly exposed side of the piece, Matthew noticed something else: "It's beautiful."

"That, too. The silvery lines are threads of iron. The sparkling material is rock crystal, or olivine. A slice of this, polished, can look like fine stained glass." They gazed at the specimen as the doctor scooped water over it and rolled it back and forth across the palm of his hand. "Well," he said finally. "Well. This is quite a find. Worth the whole journey, I'd say. Let's see if we can coax one or two more of these from our large friend."

Matthew showed the bell-shaped bump to Dr. Evans, who attacked it with enthusiasm. He wedged it off with less effort than he'd spent on the first one. The next sample—the one he'd located—didn't come as easily. He was sweating by the time it thudded to the ground. "Three is enough," he said, wiping his forehead. He wrapped two specimens carefully in his handkerchief and put them in his pocket. He held out the bell-shaped piece to Matthew.

"For me?" Matthew's hand went to it and hesitated.

"For your help and good company," the doctor said. "When we come back, there will be more of this nomad than we'll know what to do with. We shall have to bring mules in by boat. You will have to hire assistants to help you handle them."

Matthew took the piece of rock, feeling its surprising weight, its smallest bumps and indentations. He carefully put the voyager in his deepest coat pocket.

Dr. Evans climbed up on the meteorite and stood, facing one direction, then another, taking notes on landmarks and distances, drawing a crude map. Then he stepped down. "We should be on our way."

Matthew followed him down the slope, stopping to look back every few moments. The face was taking shape, and now he could imagine the force that had carved it, blasting out an eye socket, driving hard rock and earth into a ridge of nose and brow.

He wondered if he would ever see it again.

Chapter Fifteen
Mace Mullins:
July 25, Present

Isaac and I carried lawn chairs into the backyard while Phoebe led Legs out the door. She handed him a glass of iced tea. "Another inquisition?" he said.

"We'd like to know what you've got up your sleeve," Isaac said. "But mostly we're here to tell you things you need to know."

Legs cocked his head in Isaac's direction. "Things *I* need to know?"

"You told me to watch for a guy named Full Moon," l said.

Legs turned. "You saw him?"

"A big guy with a mean pig face and a circular scar on his upper right arm," I said. "Voice like sandpaper coming through a pipe."

Legs shrank into his chair.

"He told Russell he was your parole officer," Isaac said.

I related my stories, finishing with my best Full Moon

impression: "'Blind or not, he's gonna find a way to wander,'" I said, using Mullins's high-pitched, breathy voice.

Legs grimaced. "That's him." He shook his head. "All these years I've waited." He sat silent for a long time. "Go to my room, Phoebe," he said at last. "You'll find the box under my bed. Bring it out here."

A minute later she was back. She set the box down on Legs's lap. It looked different—free of mud, barely rusty.

"I had plans," Legs said. "They were put on hold seven years ago. I figured once I got out, got some real medical care, I'd be able to carry on."

"You might yet," Phoebe said, smiling cheerfully.

Legs shook his head. "The plans called for me to get back in the hills and hike trails and cross streams and sleep under old-growth cedars and breathe that wondrous air again." He sighed. "You ever heard the stories about the Port Orford Meteorite?" Legs's words raised goose bumps on my arms. The meteorite notion he'd planted in my head the day before wasn't just a *maybe* now.

He removed a key from his pocket, slipped it into the padlock, and twisted it open and off. The lid creaked when he tugged at the handle and lifted. He reached in and removed a small cloth sack wrapped with twine.

No one moved.

Legs fumbled with the twine until it loosened and fell to the grass. He handed the sack to Isaac.

Isaac felt the sack, measuring the weight and size of

its contents. I itched to get my hands on it as he reached inside. He removed a chunk of rock, three or four inches long, a couple of inches wide, smoother and darker on one side than the other. "A piece of the meteorite?" he said.

Phoebe took it. Her eyes grew wider. "It really is, isn't it," she said, and Legs nodded.

"Can I hold it?" My patience had evaporated.

Phoebe handed it over. It was heavy, like a big fishing sinker. The dark side looked as if it had been melted into one nearly smooth charcoal-hued crust, but the lighter-toned, jagged-edged side was a combination of colors and textures—spidery metallic lines zigzagging through clusters of greenish crystal-like rock. Except for the shape, it was familiar. "It's like my grandpa's rock," I said.

Legs smiled. "Same source," he said. "But your grandpa's slice has a longer history." He felt around in the box, took out a piece of paper, and handed it to me. I unfolded it. It was a photocopy, just as lame as the original that I'd found taped to Grandpa's box. I couldn't believe it.

"Matthew's map," I said. I passed it to Phoebe.

"Not much of a map, Russell," Legs said. "Your grandpa and I used to laugh about how worthless it was, although it certainly was an inspiration.

"At the time he first showed his rock and map to me, I'd already spent a lot of years walking the woods. I knew that country like I knew my backyard. I knew its trees and plants and water and rocks. Especially its rocks, which were my fascination. I knew from a mile away what kind I'd find in a particular spot. I brought rocks home, stored 'em in my basement, piled 'em in the yard, cut 'em, ground 'em down, and polished 'em.

"I'd heard the story of Dr. Evans and his meteorite, but folks didn't give it much credence when I was growing up. The hills had been searched off and on, with no result, ever since Dr. Evans made his discovery a century and a half ago. So I rarely looked for the meteorite until Art got me stoked up, and we began heading off to the mountains together.

"One day—over seven years ago, now—I was on a job for the Forest Service in an area I'd rarely visited. I'd hiked halfway up a mountainside. It was a clear day, and from a distance I noticed a round-shouldered mountain tucked behind a couple of others. I scrambled back down and talked my work partner into doing a little exploring.

"We unloaded our motorbikes from our truck and rode them on primitive trails, game trails, and no trails at all, until we couldn't ride any farther. Then we climbed up out of the forest. The puzzling thing was that we were way below the natural tree line, so there should've been trees there. But instead we were at the edge of an open space filled with rubble and fractured boulders and low-growing vegetation and a few very young and scrawny trees, maybe the height of a basketball hoop, mostly deciduous.

"And nothing else. No stumps, no signs of logging. All

around the clearing were bigger trees, conifers—mostly fir and hemlock, some cedar, a few madrona. But right there—well, it looked like someone had dropped a bomb in the middle of the forest.

"It was beginning to get dark, clouds had moved in, cold rain was falling, and my partner wanted to get back. We had a mile of rough hiking and a load of tough miles on the seat of a trail bike to get to the truck. But I convinced him to stick around." Legs shook his head. "I should've sent him back.

"We picked our way between boulders, along the bases of cliffs, over ledges, until we reached what remained of a rock upcropping. It looked like someone had taken a bite out of one side of it. But we couldn't see it that well, even up close. A clump of small birches was growing in front of it, like one of those desert oasis scenes.

"And then I saw something inside that curtain of trees. In the gloom, it looked like a giant potato that had worked its way out of the shattered earth. But we got closer, and I realized it hadn't worked its way out, it had smashed into the ground so hard it was half-buried, coated with dirt, almost like it belonged there. I was lucky to see it at all. It was a time between winter and spring. The spindly trees hadn't sprouted their leaves yet.

"I walked up and put my hand on the rock, and right away I wished I'd come alone. 'The meteorite,' my partner said. 'We've found the meteorite.' He said *we*, but

I thought, *I, I* was the one who'd searched for it for so long, *I* was the one who had the idea to venture to this mountain, *I* was the one who knew immediately what we'd found. This should've been my discovery, and Art's. But it was too late.

"Now it was near dark, and there was no way we could get that rock out of there. Not in a lifetime. Not by ourselves. But we wanted to take a piece of it with us, and I'd brought my basic rock-hounding tools—a hammer and chisel—with me, like I always did. So we pounded on the meteorite until we wedged off a chunk. The other guy dropped it in his pocket like it was his, and I went to work on one for me. It was dark and my arms were heavy, but I finally knocked off another piece.

"I had a backpack," he continued. "Day-glo orange. I emptied it and leaned it against one of the trees where we'd be sure to see it when we returned. Then we set off, stumbling down the mountain by flashlight, stopping every few minutes to map. It was slow going. Neither of us was a mapmaker, but I had a compass and watch, and I took on the duty. It was after midnight when we got back to the truck. We crept out of there, me still mapmaking, him dreaming of riches."

Legs paused again, and Isaac jumped in. "Mace Mullins?" As soon as he said it, I knew it was true.

Legs nodded.

"You didn't go back?" Phoebe said.

"We made plans. We started doing research. Whose property was it on? The feds? The state? A private party? How could we stake a claim? Get it out? Who could we talk to? How much was it worth?"

"What *was* it worth?" I said.

"We were afraid to do a lot of asking. And the money part of it wasn't the most exciting thing, not for me. It was the discovery, just knowing what we'd found. But near as we could tell from contacting a few scientists on an anonymous 'What if?' basis, it was worth millions—I don't know how many. A meteorite the size of our 'hypothetical' one was so rare that astronomers and archeologists and collectors would be tripping over each other for a chance to get a piece of it."

Isaac whistled. "It'd be worth more now."

"Yes," Legs said. "Plenty back then, though. For both of us. And for your grandpa, Russell. Art was as responsible as anyone for me finding the meteorite. I wanted to make sure he received a share once we figured out the details. But Mace got greedy. He asked me to meet him at his place one night. Wanted to go over the map, he said—redraw it so it would be fresh in our minds and make sense to both of us.

"But when I got to his cabin, Full Moon was there. He pulled a pistol, ordered me back outside. I knew if I went out, I was dead. I jumped him when he got close. We were struggling over the gun when Mace ran in and tried to help

Full Moon. By this time I had my finger on the trigger, though, and when the gun went off, Mace went down.

"When Full Moon knelt by his brother and looked up at me, there was hate in his eyes. He would've killed me right there. But I had the gun. He took off. I went home, numb with worry. The cops showed up an hour later. He'd fed them a story about walking in on me and Mace, me holding a gun, Mace on the floor.

"In spite of Full Moon's reputation, none of the authorities bought my story. Maybe if I'd said what it was the Mullins boys were after, the cops would've believed me. But I knew if I did, I'd lose the meteorite. They'd make me show 'em where it was, and they'd take it from me—not just the money, but the *feeling*.

"I hadn't told your grandpa about the meteorite yet, Russell, although I'd dropped a hint or two. I almost told him then. But he wouldn't have allowed me to go to prison. He wouldn't have been able to stay silent. He would've told the police about Mace and Full Moon. Which would've put me right back in that same dark place between heaven and hell. I decided not to tell him until we could go up there together. I'd take my chances at trial.

"I went down in flames. But I kept my mouth shut. And I kept my piece of the sky. And my map. What I didn't count on was my eyes going bad, then coming home and finding your grandpa so lost. It breaks my heart to see him like this."

"Grandpa still remembers his dreams," I said. "It's not too late for him to find out one came true."

Legs nodded. "You're right. I'll tell him." He reached into the box, slid a section of its bottom aside, and drew out an envelope. He opened it, took out a wrinkled piece of paper, and unfolded it. He thrust it in Isaac's direction. "Marines need to read maps, right? Can you figure out this one?"

Isaac looked it over and gave it back. "Maybe," he said. "With your help."

"I've got it memorized," Legs said. "But having that map in my mind is like looking at a travel brochure of a beautiful, far-off place with no money to get there. I'm ready to give up on the idea of using it myself."

I looked at the map. The paper was soft with wrinkles and seven years in the ground. It was filled with lines— heavy, light, dotted—and numbers, and times of day, and landmarks—mountains, streams, meadows, forests, clear cuts. A heavy line started at an *H* on the left side of the map near a big *W,* for *West.* It meandered east, branching off into dead ends. Just before it stopped, it split off into a thinner line that went south, then east again, almost to the other edge of the paper. There, Legs had drawn a small blackened-in circle with lines shooting off it like sunrays. Next to the circle was an *M*—for *meteorite,* I decided— and nearby was an *E,* for *East.* At the top and bottom of the paper were the letters *N* and *S.*

Compared to Matthew's map, it looked professional.

"Now that Full Moon's back," Legs said finally, "I don't have time for wishing and hoping." He leaned forward. "I need you three to help me."

"How?" Isaac said.

"I need Russell to take this box home and hide it. It's not safe here anymore."

"Sure," I said, half-chilled by fear, half-warmed by what Legs had just done. He trusted me. He trusted me with his dream.

"Then, as soon as you can, I want all of you to get up there and find the meteorite."

"By ourselves?" Phoebe said.

"If you're feeling up to it," Legs said. "Adults tend to worry and doubt and delay. They'll want to form committees and have meetings and consult lawyers. Politicians will get involved. People will get greedy."

I was convinced: no adults need apply. But I thought about Mom. Would she let me go off into the wilderness for who-knew-how-long with another kid and a half-grownup who saw ghosts?

I wasn't as concerned about Dad. Like Mom said, he was a worrier, but he worried about stuff that could happen in so-called civilization. I didn't think he'd worry about me out in the woods.

"Can you do the hiking, Isaac?" Legs said.

"If I have to walk on my hands."

Legs smiled. "Most of the trek isn't hard. But we did a lot of it on motorbikes, so even the easy part's gonna take you a while on foot."

"Mom would let me do it, if Isaac goes," Phoebe said. "She still thinks he walks on water."

"Mine will, too," I said, not at all sure.

"We'll bring it up tomorrow," Phoebe said. "Russell's mom has invited us all over for lunch. After everyone sees how nice everyone else is, it won't be a problem."

"How's your muscle, Russell?" Isaac said. "You gonna be able to work it hard?"

"If I have to walk on my hands." Brave words. I didn't feel quite so brave.

"You can go quick—maybe the day after tomorrow," Legs said. "Be out of here before Full Moon knows what's happening. Get one of your moms to drive you up Sixes River Road to the thirty-mile mark. The road's mostly dirt—at least it was—but it's okay this time of year. That'll save you a couple days walking."

"The *H* on the map," Isaac said. "That's the coast highway—101?"

"You're gonna do fine with this map, son," Legs said. "The *H* is where the Sixes River Road intersects 101."

"My mom would drive," I said. "If she lets me go."

"Isaac and I will talk to our mom ahead of time," Phoebe said. "Once she says yes, we'll be ready for yours."

I imagined the possibilities if Mom said yes—a long

hike in the wilderness with Phoebe and Isaac, seeing stuff I'd never seen before, tracking down the giant meteorite, showing the evidence to Legs.

But what if we couldn't find the meteorite? Got lost? Ran out of food? Maybe Mom saying no wouldn't be so bad after all. I'd be home with her, comfortable and safe.

But would I really want to stay behind when I had the chance to bring back something amazing to show Grandpa, something to wake him up and make him care and help him connect with the real world—and me—again?

Mom had to say yes. She *had* to.

Grandpa had installed wood cabinets high on the garage walls, above open shelves of assorted rocks, some polished smooth, some fresh-picked rough. None looked like the mantel rock.

I climbed the stepladder and unlocked a cabinet door. It squawked open. I pushed aside dead flies and cobwebs and enough of Grandpa's fishing gear to make a space, then set Legs's box on a shelf.

I looked over my shoulder as I snapped the lock shut, fighting a feeling that someone was watching. But Mom was at the store, shopping for the next day's lunch. No one was in the garage. Or the driveway, I saw, as I reached the bottom of the ladder. Or the yard, or the street. For a moment I wondered if Full Moon knew where I lived. Then I pushed away the thought, like dead flies and cobwebs.

Chapter Sixteen

For the Mantel:
July 26-27, Present

I'd worried about how Isaac would act at lunch the next day. I was afraid something would set him off again. But I shouldn't have been concerned. He shone like the California sun, acting all normal and grownup. He smooth-talked the moms, convincing them we needed a whole seven days for our adventure—a hike to experience the beauty of the coastal range while the good summer weather was at its peak. He blinded them with his brilliance. Mom even agreed, after clearing the whole thing with Dad in a quick phone conversation, to drive us to the trailhead. This was almost going to be too easy. No one mentioned the meteorite. Or Full Moon Mullins.

Isaac and Phoebe picked me up early the next morning for our supply run. At the hardware store we spent some of our money and some we'd gotten from Legs on the backpacking supplies on our list, including the best of the gross-looking freeze-dried meals. Then we drove to

Sullivan's Super Duper for more food.

We tore our grocery list in thirds and split up. We filled the cart with stuff that wouldn't weigh us down, that would last a week in the mountains—dehydrated soups, powdered milk, cocoa, dried fruit, cheese, bread, nuts, raisins, trail mix, energy bars. I picked out six apples, promising to make room for them in my pack.

Isaac and Phoebe started for the car with most of the groceries while I waited at the checkout counter for change. As I looked out the store's big front window, a familiar brown car pulled into the parking lot.

I held my breath while the pig-mobile eased into a space on the opposite side of the lot. How had Full Moon known? Or had he just gotten lucky?

I watched. Full Moon sat. Did Phoebe and Isaac know the oink-man was there? Five minutes earlier they'd been joking around, laughing. Now they looked all business as they loaded groceries into the trunk.

"Your change," the clerk said impatiently, like it wasn't the first time. I pocketed the money, picked up two bags of groceries, and headed to the car. Trying to look cool and unconcerned, I put the bags in the trunk and got in the back seat behind Phoebe. Isaac started the engine and headed toward the exit.

"Full Moon's here," I said. "Parked."

"We thought so," Phoebe said.

"There's no reason for him to think we're shopping for

a trip to the mountains," Isaac said. "For all he knows, we're buying everyday groceries. Right?"

"What if he talks to the clerk?" Phoebe said.

"Then we're in trouble," Isaac said. "I went to school with Debbie Milton. Telling her something is like putting it on a billboard."

We were out on the street now, moving past Full Moon's parked car.

"But it doesn't matter," Isaac said. "He won't know where or when we're going. We just have to be sure we're not followed when we leave."

"At least he didn't see us at the hardware store," Phoebe said.

"We didn't see *him*," I said. "It doesn't mean he didn't see *us*."

"Let's hope he's still got Legs on his mind," Isaac said. "If he doesn't see Legs leave, maybe he'll hang around here forever."

As we turned onto Phoebe's street, she gasped.

In front of the house sat a police car and an ambulance, lights flashing.

Isaac swore under his breath. "Legs," he said.

Grandpa, I thought.

Becky met us just inside, her face flushed. I heard voices coming from the direction of Legs's room.

"It's Legs, honey," Becky said, taking Phoebe in her arms.

"What's wrong with him?" Phoebe's words came out muffled by her mom's shoulder. Isaac headed for Legs's room, but I hung back, waiting for the answer.

"I found him in bed," Becky said. "I couldn't wake him. The medics haven't been able to wake him."

"He's dead?" Phoebe pulled back and looked at her mom.

"Not dead, honey. But not good. Unconscious."

I heard Isaac's voice from Legs's room, asking questions. I heard the word *diabetes*. Finally a uniformed woman and man hurried out, carrying Legs on a stretcher. He looked like a ghost, floating past with a white sheet covering everything but his pale face. A policeman came down the hall and stopped. His nametag said "Howard Dexter, Chief." He waited for Becky to notice him. Outside, doors slammed. An engine sparked to life. A siren growled low and rose to a scream that faded as the ambulance raced away.

"I'm not a doctor, Becky," Chief Dexter said. "But the medics assume the diabetes is what got him. You say he's near-blind. Means his blood vessels are messed up. So we're thinking heart attack or stroke. Or he could be in a diabetic coma."

Isaac came out of Legs's room and leaned against the wall. His face was shadowed by that far-off look again.

"He hasn't exactly been a boy scout," the chief continued, "but I'm sure the docs will do what they can."

Becky jerked away from the chief. "Why wouldn't they?" Her voice quavered. "I have to go check on Art. He's out in the backyard, probably wondering what's going on." Halfway across the dining room, she stopped. "You can let yourself out, Dex." She turned and hurried on.

The chief shrugged and walked out.

I could feel my eyes welling up. Phoebe's face was teary. All the excitement over our trip had disappeared, replaced by concern for Legs.

"I've never seen anyone in a diabetic coma," Isaac said. "Or someone who's had a stroke. But I've seen guys whose lights had been dimmed for them. Our side, their side. I still see their faces.

"Chief Dexter has spent his whole career giving out speeding tickets," Isaac continued. "He doesn't know natural causes from night visitors."

"What do you mean?" Phoebe said.

"I mean I felt something when I walked into Legs's room. Someone had been there."

"But who?" Phoebe whispered. "You mean Full Moon?"

Isaac nodded.

"You didn't see anything?" I said. "Blood? Bruises? Lumps?"

"His clothes were scattered."

"That's not much," I said.

"Still . . ." Isaac said. "The whole thing doesn't smell right."

"Why would Full Moon hurt Legs?" I said. "He's the only one who knows how to find the meteorite."

"Maybe the moon-man got impatient," Isaac said. "Maybe he came looking for the map and Legs woke up and reason flew out the window and they went at it."

"Maybe Full Moon decided Legs had passed the map on to someone else," Phoebe said.

I fought down a fluttery feeling; the someone else was *me*. "When would he have gotten in?"

"Anytime during the night," Phoebe said. "We usually don't lock the door."

I had never lived in a place where people didn't lock their doors. I thought about where we were going. Out in the middle of the wilderness, there would be no doors. "Did you say anything to the cop?" I asked Isaac.

"No."

"Shouldn't we?" Phoebe said.

Isaac shrugged. "All we have is the paranoia of a war-scarred wreck, some would say. Chief Dexter, for instance."

"What if Full Moon really did it?" Phoebe said. "By the time we say anything, it could be too late."

"It's already too late," I said. "Legs is in the hospital."

"What would he want us to do?" Isaac said.

I swallowed a lump of sadness, coated with fear. "Go find the meteorite."

"I think so, too," Isaac said. "Phoebe?"

"That piece of the sky is his life," she said. "He'd want us up in his hills."

"It's unanimous, then," I said.

"Let's get packing," Isaac said.

But first I headed for the backyard. Legs had planned to tell Grandpa about the meteorite, but now he couldn't. Someone had to. I found Grandpa sitting in a chair and knelt down next to him. "You know Phoebe and Isaac, Grandpa?"

He didn't say yes, but at least he was looking at me, and there was some curiosity in his eyes.

"I'm going to the mountains with them." I noticed my voice growing louder, as if that would help him understand. "Before Legs went to prison, he found the lost meteorite. He wanted to tell you, but he couldn't. He gave us a map so we could find it."

Grandpa continued to stare. For a long moment I thought I might as well be talking to the fence. But then he took my hand. "Great-Grandpa Matthew's meteorite?" he said.

I took a deep breath and nodded.

"His piece of the sky?" His eyes were wet with remembering now. "Legs found it?"

"Yes."

"You're going up to find it . . . Russell?"

My heart swelled. I couldn't remember the last time he'd said my name. "We're going to try. But you can't say anything to anyone."

He nodded and put his forefinger to his lips. "I could have helped once." He looked at the back of his hand, wrinkled and veined and spotted. "Now I'm too old. But you're young. And you don't need me. You just need to remember what I taught you."

"You'll be with me anyway, Grandpa," I said. "I'll be thinking of you the whole time."

He smiled, warm and lively. "Bring me back a piece, will you? For the mantel."

I squeezed his gnarled hand. I didn't want to let go, but I had somewhere I had to be. I had something I had to bring him. "A big piece, Grandpa," I said.

He squeezed back, the kind of squeeze that told me we were connected by more than skin and blood. He knew me, he knew where he was, and he knew what I was talking about.

I'd do anything for him, I decided. A little trip to the mountains? No problem. Bringing back a chunk of lost meteorite that almost no one else has been able to find? Easy. Staying out of the path of a murderous criminal who wants the same thing we do? No sweat.

I got up and gave him a hug and turned away quickly. I didn't want to see the light fade from his eyes.

Chapter Seventeen

On the Trail:
July 27, Present

Four hours later, after an easy five miles of smooth Sixes River Road pavement and a slow and bumpy twenty-five of back-country dirt and steep nerve-jangling dropoffs, Mom delivered us to our starting point, the middle of nowhere.

I turned and waved one last time as she started back.

Ahead of us lay a narrow logging road, two brown tracks overhung by shrubby growth and trees. Isaac and Phoebe moved out, Isaac taking one rut, Phoebe the other. She already had her music plugged into her ears. Their packs were stuffed full, topped with sleeping bags. I followed, shifting Grandpa's pack on my back, getting it just right. How long would it be before it began to wear me down? I lengthened my stride, testing my leg. So far, so good.

This spur road looked rough—a narrow alley of pot-holed washboard dirt—but according to the map it was still part of the route that Legs and Mace had covered in their truck. Five miles of this, then twenty-one miles of an intersecting logging road, then seven to ten miles of the rugged and now probably overgrown trail Legs and Mace had done on their bikes. Then came the tough part—finding the right place to leave the trail, heading off into the woods with no path, maybe no good landmarks, bushwhacking five miles or more through undergrowth and trees with nothing but the map, a compass, and whatever our senses might whisper to us. I was glad this wasn't my first time in the wilderness; my trips with Grandpa had to have taught me something about finding my way and perseverance and listening to my instincts. And survival.

Isaac and Phoebe slowed and looked back, waiting for me, but just as I was about to pick up my pace and show them I was no slug from the city, I felt something hard and pointy land in the back of my shoe and slip under my heel. My next step was painful. I wouldn't be going anywhere until I did some excavation work.

I stopped. "Go ahead!" I yelled to them. "I've got something in my shoe! I'll catch up!" Isaac waved, and they kept going, more like strolling than hiking. I found a big rock and sat, making sure the weight of my pack didn't pull me over backwards. The quiet was overwhelming as I untied my shoe, slipped it off, and dumped out a raisin-sized stone that had felt more like prune-sized.

As I hurried to get my shoe back on, I heard something through the dense woods behind me. A bird song was replaced by other sounds—the poke-along idle of an engine, maybe, the crunch-hiss of tires on gravel and dirt. Mom coming back? Why would she? I looked up the road. Phoebe and Isaac had disappeared around a bend. Why had I told them to go on?

The sounds stopped. The bird resumed its singing. I'd imagined the whole thing, probably. But as I listened and stared and got to my feet, a thin cloud of dust drifted through the trees and swirled away.

Then there was nothing. No dust, no engine or tire or door-shutting sounds, no sign of anyone on the road behind me. Just the bird, the buzz of insects, the whisper of wind in the trees. And my imagination, I decided, turned up to full volume.

Even if it really was a car, there was no reason to think Full Moon was behind the wheel. Anyone could drive these dirt roads; Legs himself had done it for years.

So why couldn't I get the image of Full Moon's face out of my head?

I shrugged my pack into place and took off. I accelerated around a curve and caught sight of Phoebe and Isaac, not far ahead.

Should I tell them what I'd heard? Seen? What *had* it been, exactly? I decided to say nothing, at least for now.

"I figure ten miles today," Isaac said. "It's two-thirty. We've got five hours before the light starts failing. So we only have to average a couple miles an hour."

"How far tomorrow?" I said.

"Twenty," Isaac said. "The first sixteen should be kind of like this—a walk in the park. The last four we'll be on Legs's bike trail. A challenge, maybe."

"Day three?" Phoebe said.

"Difficult. Somewhere between eight and eleven, probably. Legs didn't know exactly how far they went on bike and foot."

We moved along, mostly up. The road wound south, often through thick dark woods but sometimes into meadows and clear cuts and areas of new tree growth—stubby evergreens, lanky birches. From time to time I found myself looking back.

It was just after four o'clock when we reached what we thought was the intersecting logging road pictured on the map, the place where we needed to make our first turn.

"You puppies are doing good," Isaac said. He got the map out of his backpack and studied it and our surroundings, then let Phoebe and me look. We were a little ahead of schedule, but the road matched, the terrain matched.

As we started down the cutoff, I looked back one more time. Nothing. I felt better.

At four-thirty we stopped for water and a snack and a few minutes without weight on our backs. The crackers and cheese tasted like Sunday dinner.

"Much lighter," Phoebe joked as she shouldered her pack again.

Isaac downed a pill. "Shedding those ounces makes a difference over the long haul."

I hoped so. My shoulders were already complaining. Soon I'd be glad for every ounce I could shed.

The afternoon wore on. We were still moving up most of the time, and east, the setting sun at our backs. We stopped for a long drink of water every hour, replacing what we'd sweated out.

At about eight o'clock we reached a spot where the road bent to the right around the base of a hill. On the side of the road, a stream cut through a clearing and then dropped into a stand of white-barked trees with dark shiny leaves.

"I think we've found home for the night," Isaac said, and I silently yelled a cheer for our leader.

We located a dry, level spot in the clearing and set our packs on the trunk of a fallen tree. While Isaac started a fire, Phoebe and I went to the stream. We knelt on the sand and stones and filled our small aluminum pots with clear, icy water. I set mine on a flat rock and splashed my face with cold. I looked over and watched Phoebe do the same, then gulp a long drink from her cupped hands.

"Whoa!" I said. "We have to filter it first."

"I was thirsty."

"Use your canteen."

"It's warm."

"You wanna get sick?"

"Look at this water. Could it be cleaner?"

We went back to the campsite, where Isaac had a fire going. He was in the middle of lighting his backpacking stove.

"Your stubborn little sister thinks she's a horsey," I said. "She was slurping water from the stream."

Phoebe stuck out her tongue at me. "Tattler."

"You're asking for trouble, Phoebs," Isaac said. "Invisible critters live in mountain water."

"Little bugs," I said. "Country girls are supposed to know about stuff like that."

"Country girls aren't afraid of bugs," Phoebe said.

We managed to finish dinner—freeze-dried macaroni and cheese—before complete dark, but by the time we'd cleaned up and I'd gone for more water, stars were blooming over the treetops. Firelight danced on our sleeping bags rolled out on fir boughs.

I pulled on a sweatshirt and sat close to the fire. Phoebe sat across from me, trying to avoid smoke.

"Where's Isaac?" I said.

"Went for a walk, he said."

"Like we haven't already had one."

"He's afraid Full Moon's following us."

"Where'd you come up with that?" I said, but I couldn't shake the same fear. Nobody had mentioned it, but we could smell it on each other.

Isaac strolled into camp a few minutes later. His face told no stories.

"I can see why Legs loved it up here," Phoebe said cheerfully. "Listen. All you hear is the campfire crackling. All you smell is mountain air and wood smoke."

"The sky's alive with stars," I said. I thought about my grandpa and my great-great-great-grandpa, looking at these same stars from this same place.

"Can you imagine what it must've looked like up here when Legs's meteorite came screaming down?" Isaac said.

I tried to imagine it. Looking up at that sky, anything seemed possible.

Isaac sat down by the fire. A leg of his jeans rode up, revealing the tip of a leather knife sheath above his boot.

I stopped thinking about stars and meteorites. I was back on Earth, thinking about Full Moon.

Chapter Eighteen

James: September 14, 1861

J ames heard the dog bark, just outside the door, but it wasn't his let-me-in bark. It was the go-away-strange-critter bark he used on mountain lions, bears, porcupines, skunks, and any living thing he thought might be too much to tackle. James tried to ignore the distraction. He needed to get this lesson—a long and difficult piece by Washington Irving—memorized by the next day.

The dog barked again, louder, more urgent. "Jupiter!" James yelled. But Jupiter paid no attention, barking ceaselessly.

What if trouble really had come calling? Eyeing the rifle mounted on the wall, James got up and opened the door wide enough to look out, wide enough for Jupiter to slip in if he wanted.

Dusk was settling through the trees. A stranger stood at the edge of the yard, looking as if he would like to come closer. His clothes—stovepipe hat, velvet-collared chesterfield, shiny half boots—seemed more fit for church than a walk from town.

James stepped onto the porch and grabbed Jupiter by the scruff of the neck. "Hush!"

"Will he eat me?" A smile showed through the man's beard.

"That depends."

The man laughed. "Are you James?"

James hesitated. "Who are you?"

"I talked to your mother at her store. She said I could find you here."

"Why would you want to?"

"She said if questions were to be asked, I might meet my match."

James felt himself smiling. He knelt and scratched Jupiter's chest. "He's a friend," he whispered in the dog's black ear. "Come in," he said to the man.

The stranger greeted the dog with an outstretched hand, then offered his other hand to James. They went inside, where James lit a whale-oil lamp and took the man's hat and coat. They sat across from each other at the table, Jupiter curled up on the floor nearby.

"My name is Charles Jackson," the visitor said. "Dr. Charles Jackson. I traveled here on behalf of the Boston Society of Natural History to track down the origins of an interesting geological specimen." He leaned forward, eyes searching James's eyes.

"Approximately five years ago, a scientist named Dr. John Evans came through this area," Dr. Jackson continued. "He set off from your town to explore the country between here and Eugene City." He studied James for another moment. "How old would you have been then?"

James did a quick subtraction. "About eight."

"Dr. Evans hired your brother Matthew to guide him and his two companions and handle the mules. Do you remember that?"

"I do," James said. "I missed him so much. He tolerates every question I ask. When he left, my mother soon tired of them."

"He's gone again."

"Fighting with the Union Army."

"So your mother said. A brave young man."

"I'd trade his bravery for his presence."

"Did he ever talk with you about his journey?"

"Hard, he said, but worth the effort. He often talked about Dr. Evans returning and taking him back to the mountains."

"Dr. Evans did come back to the Oregon Territory in '58, but we don't believe he journeyed to Port Orford."

"Matthew would have said so."

"He had plans to return here recently," Dr. Jackson said. "Unfortunately, he fell ill. He died."

Dr. Evans was dead? James had a hard time digesting the news. What would Matthew think?

"Do you know why he wanted to come back?" Dr. Jackson said.

"I cannot guess."

"Matthew never told you of discoveries?"

"He told me of sweat and blisters and stubborn animals."

"Yet he wanted to return with the doctor?"

"He also spoke of star-filled nights, wildflowers, rivers as clear as the air and teeming with fish, and wild animals as tame as Jupiter."

The doctor's gaze grew more intense. "Dr. Evans made an important finding on his journey, James. A large rock, half-buried in the earth, possibly weighing ten tons or more. He chipped away a sample and later sent the specimen to Boston, where I had the good fortune to examine it."

"A rock is hardly an oddity," James said. "My mother has me digging them from our garden as if they were potatoes."

"Ah, but this was a special rock. This one came from far, far away. From out of the stars your brother mentioned. It was a meteorite, one of the largest ever discovered."

"A meteorite." James let the word cool on his tongue like hot soup.

"Yes. Very rare. Very valuable. And unfortunately, very lost."

"Lost?"

"As I said, Dr. Evans died recently. His journal of the trip contained references to the route, and it was believed that following the descriptions in the journal, along with information he later provided to me, would lead us to the site. But attempts to locate it have proven fruitless. We thought perhaps your brother could help."

"I'm sure he would." Suddenly James could see a way of bringing Matthew home. "If you could talk to his officers, maybe they would allow him to leave the Army. He could return to Port Orford and help you find the meteorite himself."

Dr. Jackson smiled. He said he might just do that, if the Boston Society of Natural History officials could convince the Army that Matthew was needed more on a trip of exploration than fighting against the rebels. He wrote down information about Matthew in a small leather notebook.

At the door he handed James a card with his name and address in Boston, and the name and address of the Society. "I gave one of these to your mother, but I would like you to have one also. If you think of anything your brother told you about his journey, please write to me or have your mother send me a telegram. Any expenses will be covered, and there could be money in it for you."

"Yes, sir."

Jupiter saw the doctor to the gate, where he put on his tall hat and waved goodbye. He turned and headed down the road toward town.

James returned to the house, picked up the lamp from the table, and went into his small bedroom. At the far corner of the room, he knelt with the lamp at his side. He fished a jackknife out of his pocket, wedged its strongest blade against the butt of a short plank, and pried it loose.

He reached into the shallow space beneath it.

He felt it—the soft cloth of the sack, the weight of its contents. He loosened the drawstring and gently wrapped his fingers around the rock, sensing its cool roughness, lifting it out into the flickering light. With his thumb and forefinger he silhouetted its bell shape against the window, imagining it traveling through space for millions of miles before streaking through Earth's blue heavens and crashing into the side of the mountain.

Matthew had shown James the rock—a piece of the sky, he called it—many times, told tales of its discovery, left it here for James's safekeeping, warned him to tell no one. The meteorite it had come from belonged to nobody but Dr. Evans, Matthew said, and until the doctor and Matthew and a huge but loyal company of men and pack animals went back to drag it whole or in pieces from the mountain where it rested, it would remain concealed.

But Matthew hadn't ever told James where they'd found it, not exactly. Perhaps he didn't remember. Wouldn't it be grand, though, if Dr. Jackson could free Matthew from the Army and enlist his help in finding the meteorite again? And now James was old enough to go along.

He pictured himself leading a team of mules up a wilderness trail: Ahead, Matthew and Dr. Jackson and other important men walk into a clearing, where Matthew points into the distance at a bald mountain. "There," he says. "There's where you'll find your meteorite." There is much excitement and hand-shaking and congratulating as Matthew invites James to walk with him at the front of the party, and they step off together.

Chapter Nineteen

Precautions:
July 28, Present

Daylight and bird songs woke me after a mostly restful night. But I remembered waking once before, seeing the empty sleeping bag next to me and lying awake, heart drumming, until Isaac returned.

After a hurried breakfast of peanut butter on graham crackers, string cheese, and dried fruit, we broke camp and moved out. I felt sore in the shoulders and stiff in the back, but a few miles would iron out those kinks. My leg still felt okay.

Lack of rain had left a layer of dust on the road. I looked back and saw our footprints trailing us like signposts. There was no good way to cover our tracks. So we plodded on, taking breaks when Isaac suggested it or when someone picked up a rock in a shoe or needed a trip to the trees.

"Lunch," Isaac grunted at last when we came to a shaded clearing. We sat, Phoebe and I facing the route ahead, rolling hill after rolling hill. Isaac faced back.

"You think he's there?" I said. I wanted Isaac to answer no, but his night patrols, the knife strapped to his leg, the size of the hunting knife belted to his side, said something different.

"Just being cautious," Isaac said. He gave me a little headshake, warning me away from the topic, but I decided it was time to go public.

"I heard something when we started out," I said. "When you guys were ahead of me on the trail." I told them about the car sounds, the dust.

"What would Full Moon do?" Phoebe said, wide-eyed, and part of me wished I had my little might-have-happened story back.

"Don't worry about it, Phoebs," Isaac said. "What Russell heard—if he *did* hear it—could've been anyone. Full Moon's probably back in Port Orford, wondering what happened to his spy." Which wasn't exactly a comforting thought. Would Pig-face try to find out from my mom, or Phoebe's?

We took another break at three-thirty. Isaac looked over the map while Phoebe and I peered over his shoulder. He did some calculations on a separate piece of paper. "I figure our actual walking time has been about seven hours," he said. "I counted my strides for the last fifteen minutes, figured two-and-a-half feet per stride, multiplied it out, and came up with an hourly distance." He circled a number on the paper. "We're logging almost two-and-a-quarter miles per hour. Which means we've covered more than fifteen miles today. You guys are *animals.*"

"We're doing okay?" The thought made me feel safer for a moment. If we kept up this pace, Full Moon, older for sure and out of shape, maybe, could be struggling.

"So far," Isaac said. "Which is good. Once we make the next turn, it could be like walking through quicksand."

We started off again, saying little. Everyone's attention was on the landmarks—the hills. But the hills looked pretty much the same. Finally, a wooden bridge took us across a stream. A clear-cut climbed up a hill to the north, and we found it on the map, which also showed, in another half-mile or so, a dead fir tree, blackened by lightning. A hundred yards beyond that was a boulder that marked the beginning of the trail. Would any of it still be there more than seven years later?

We trudged on. The road curved and narrowed. Lack of use had allowed forest and undergrowth to close in on both sides, and from time to time we had to walk single file to avoid getting hung up or scraped by branches or stickers.

"The snag," Isaac said.

I sidestepped left to see better. And there it was, whitened by age, blackened by heat, rising like a steeple. The dead fir.

We kept walking, searching for the boulder. The map didn't say how far off the road it was, and now it could be harder to spot, obscured by years of Mother Nature's work.

"Bingo," Isaac said.

I looked, but even after Phoebe whispered, "I see it," I saw only trees and shrubs and shadow. Then the shape emerged, a gray, car-sized block of smooth rock fifteen feet from the road. "Me, too," I said.

"Start walking again," Isaac said. "Same pace, same stride."

"But the boulder," I said. "It's where we turn."

"Patience, Muscle," Isaac said. "We're going to leave a false track."

He led us down the road to a small clearing on our left. We veered into the tall grass and doubled back, trying to tread lightly, skirting the road, then giant-stepping to the strip of growth that separated the ruts, and to the other grassy edge.

"I think I see what's left of a trail," Isaac said when we neared the boulder. "Trees on either side, but down the middle's a corridor of just low-growing stuff."

I looked. Isaac was right. Just past the boulder a skinny alley showed, cutting off through the forest. But the going wouldn't be easy.

"So far, so good, Legs," Isaac murmured, reaching back and pulling a dark-bladed machete from his backpack. Legs had included the big knife on his list of necessities, and he'd been right. Isaac shouldered the blunt edge of the blade and moved forward, struggling over and around fallen limbs and growth.

"Why don't you chop down some of this stuff for us?" Phoebe asked with her loud, I'm-plugged-in voice.

"Soon." Isaac held his forefinger to his lips. "I don't wanna make our entry point obvious."

"Oh," Phoebe said, and again I looked back.

"Keep your voice down, Phoebs," Isaac said.

We snaked and stumbled single file up and down the trail. Some of the path was clear and easy to navigate, some of it was thick with assorted weeds and bushes and young trees that made the going difficult.

My backpack snagged a thick branch of a sticker bush. I struggled to free it. "Hold up a minute," I said.

"Let's take a break," Isaac said.

I pulled my pack loose. I felt a twinge of pain at the side of my forehead.

A deep pain in my calf.

"You're bleeding," Phoebe said.

I touched my temple and stared at the smudge on my finger. "Stickers."

She poured a handful of water from her canteen and splashed it over the cut.

"I'll put something on that when we stop," Isaac said.

"It's just a scratch," I said. "I barely felt it."

Phoebe took a long drink. She found a log and sat. No one talked. I settled beside her while Isaac studied the map. "It looks like we've got about two more miles of woods," he said. "Then the trail crosses a stream and works its way up to an open area where we could check our bearings."

"Two miles might take a while in this stuff," I said, kneading my calf with my knuckles.

"You're right, Muscle. I'll try to clear a path." He picked up the machete and swept it through the air, slicing through a tangle of thorny growth. "If Full Moon gets this deep on the trail, it means he has a fix on us, anyway."

We went quiet. Listening. But all I heard was the chatter of a bird, a breeze in the branches overhead.

Phoebe bent over to retie her shoe. When she didn't straighten back up, I got curious. "What's wrong?"

"My stomach's a little crampy," she admitted, standing up at last.

I thought about the stream water. She took another swig from the canteen. She tried to smile.

Chapter Twenty

Night Watch:
July 28-29, Present

We started off again, Isaac leading the way, clearing aside obstacles with the machete. And the going got easier, at least for Phoebe and me. Which was good. My calf had begun to pester me steadily, as if a small, mean-tempered dog was nipping at it. Every time I had to go over or under something, I waited for the muscle to break down. Then what?

But what about Isaac? He was moving better, trying hard to march like a Marine, but not many days before he'd been half-lame. And while Phoebe and I were running our road miles, he was sleeping or sitting or taking his mind-numbing, body-numbing pills. How could he keep going? How long could he hold up as the trailblazer after being the night watchman, too?

I'd keep moving, no matter how bad my leg got.

By a half-hour later, Phoebe must have sensed that Isaac needed a break. "Can I lead for a while?" she asked. I was surprised. She seemed to be hurting. She wasn't walking as tall. She was breathing harder. She answered questions with one-note grunts.

"I'm in a rhythm, Phoebs," Isaac said. "Maybe tomorrow."

We kept on, me listening for the stream. It was something to distract me from the monotony of putting one foot in front of the other over and over. Maybe it had dried up, or changed course, or maybe we weren't on the right trail.

Finally I heard something. But it wasn't running water.

From somewhere behind us, sharp and unmistakable, came the sound of a breaking branch.

Isaac stopped. He motioned for Phoebe and me to pass him. All of a sudden my leg quit mattering. All of a sudden I wanted to run.

"It could be nothing," Isaac whispered. "A deer, a falling limb. But I want you guys to work about a hundred yards ahead with the machete. Then double back to fifty yards and get off the trail. Twenty feet or so. Far enough that you're not going to be seen, close enough that you're not going to get lost. Okay?"

"What are you gonna do?" Phoebe said.

"I'll wait. Out of sight. If you don't see me in fifteen minutes, you'll probably be seeing someone else. Let him go by. Then hustle back down the trail. If I don't catch up with you, ditch everything you don't need and head for home. When you sleep, sleep off the trail. I don't think he'll come after you, because he'll expect me to have the map, and if he gets me, he'll have it."

I couldn't believe I was hearing this. "We'll just stay with you."

"Get moving," Isaac said. "I'll be along in a few minutes."

Phoebe paled. "What do you mean, 'If he gets me?'"

Isaac ignored the question. He switched off Phoebe's music, yanked her earbuds, unclipped her player, and stuffed it all in her backpack. "We need your ears."

I took the machete. We started off. I looked back once as Isaac melted into the woods.

"This is stupid," Phoebe said. "We should stay with him." But I kept going. Isaac knew what he was doing; Isaac had been to war.

We covered what we agreed was a hundred yards and then went a bit farther, me cutting through enough growth to leave a fresh path for whoever came after us. Then we headed back and veered off into the trees. We shed our packs and ducked behind a big fallen fir. We couldn't see the trail, but we knew where it was.

I listened. Bird songs started, stopped, started again. My nose filled with smells, familiar and unfamiliar—trees and moss and fungus and plants and damp earth. My own sweat.

"What's Isaac gonna do?" Phoebe whispered.

"I don't know."

"He has two knives."

"He won't use 'em," I said, trying to calm her fears. And mine.

This was taking forever. I checked my watch. The minute hand had crept eight tiny spaces. I couldn't believe we were here, at the mercy of a guy like Full Moon. Why had we come? I listened to my heart thump out the answer: *stupid-stupid-stupid.*

We'd made plans, but we hadn't planned for this. Once we'd suspected how desperate Full Moon was, we should've just cooled it and waited for him to go away. Or we could've gone to the cops. Maybe whoever eventually led the search for the meteorite would've let all of us— Legs, even—come along.

I pulled my cell phone from my pack and switched it on. No signal.

"You think he's up here?" Phoebe whispered.

"I don't know. I thought we did a good job of covering our trail."

She shrugged, unconvinced. "My stomach feels worse." She got out her canteen, took a swig, and made a face. "Warm."

I passed up the chance to remind her that she'd had her cold water, fresh from the stream, that maybe it was the cause of her stomach problem. She leaned back against a tree and pointed at her wrist.

I checked my watch. "Eleven minutes." I turned my attention to the path. Blinking sweat out of my eyes, I raised up enough to see where we'd come from.

Nothing. That was good news, wasn't it? If Isaac and Full Moon were tangling somewhere, even fifty yards away, wouldn't I see or hear some sign of the struggle?

"I heard something," Phoebe said a few moments later. "A hiss, like a snake."

I heard it too. Not a snake, but somebody trying to get our attention. From the direction of the trail. "Don't answer," I whispered, and Phoebe frowned at me, like, *What idiot would?*

"Phoebs!" Isaac's voice called. "Muscle!"

I took my first deep breath in fifteen minutes.

"Over here," Phoebe said, struggling to her feet.

We made our way back to the path. "No sign of him," Isaac said. "Which doesn't mean he's not back there. But for now at least, he's not riding in our pockets. You okay, Phoebs?"

"Don't say I told you so, but my stomach's churning."

"Can you go on?"

"Walking feels okay, so far."

"You lead the way," he told me. "I'm gonna hang back, keep an eye on Phoebs, watch our rear." He smiled as I took a swing at a stray sticker branch and missed. "We'll keep our distance."

When we got past the section of trail we'd already

covered, I began hacking a wider path. Phoebe's face had taken on the pasty, puffy look of some of the crescent-shaped fungus growing on nearby tree trunks. Once she blurted out, "Wait!" and shed her backpack, heading for the woods.

"Feel better?" Isaac asked when she returned.

She nodded and shouldered her pack and started off again, but she didn't look better. She looked worse. I thought about what was coming. This trail wasn't good, but at least it was a trail. The next day we'd be forging our own way. Could Phoebe make it?

I listened to her labored breathing. Isaac asked her if she wanted to rest or even stop for the night, but she said no.

So we walked on, me wielding the machete, leaving a trail of cuttings and dangling branches. Phoebe's face shone with sweat. Limp wisps of hair stuck to her forehead. Her ponytail drooped. She stopped and dropped her pack and hurried off into the trees again. When she came back, moving like something nasty was gnawing at her stomach, Isaac had her pack strapped to his chest. He kept it there, even when she begged for it.

Finally, when the sun had sunk low and the air had cooled, the trail took us out to a clearing that ended at a high bluff, dropping off to a rocky canyon far below.

"A good place to stop for the night." Isaac got no arguments. We'd collected more water thirty minutes back, and he didn't mention it, but the clearing was wide enough that Full Moon would have to cross a lot of open space—a hundred yards or more—to get to us.

Phoebe sat on a patch of grass, her back against a thick log, her eyes half-closed, while Isaac and I set up camp. We started a fire and emptied the canteens into a pot for boiling.

I offered Phoebe crackers, but she shook her head. "I can't."

"Nibble one," Isaac said. "I'll get some soup going for you. You need something back in your stomach."

She took a cracker. Five minutes later, I looked and saw one small corner gone. Her breathing was shallow, as if she didn't want to disturb the balance keeping her insides in check.

My legs felt rubbery, but I didn't want to sit. I walked to the edge of the cliff and looked down. A narrow, brushy ledge jutted out ten feet below, but beyond that was a vast nothingness. Trees at the bottom of the drop—tall old evergreens—barely reached to the ankles of the steep rock wall. An empty, tumbling feeling rose in my stomach, and I quickly stepped back.

I watched the sun drop behind the hills, then walked back to the fire. While Phoebe sipped soup from a metal cup, Isaac hovered over her. She nibbled more of the cracker.

I peeled an apple and gave her a chunk.

"Thanks." She took a small bite. "Good."

The bread in my backpack was smashed, the cheese was

warm and oily, but the sandwiches I made for myself and Isaac tasted like Mom's home cookin'.

Isaac made instant coffee. "Want a cup, Muscle?"

"Sure." I'd never tried coffee before. I held the cup under my nose, waiting for some of the heat to go away. When I finally took a sip, I was surprised at how it tasted. I almost liked it, and I drank steadily until it was gone.

Phoebe struggled to her feet and started for the nearest trees. Isaac went with her most of the way. When they returned, she brought back the stink of puke. She sank to the ground again and leaned against the log, eyes closed.

"You can say it now, guys," she said.

"What?" I said.

"I told you so."

"You'll be better in the morning," Isaac said.

I went to the trees with the machete, eyes and ears on alert, and hacked down boughs for mattresses. But aside from small animals and birds, I didn't hear or see anything. I was beginning to feel better. Maybe Full Moon wasn't following us, after all.

Phoebe was in her bag, eyes closed, when I returned for the last time. Isaac was loading wood on the fire. Sparks flew into the starry sky.

"She's cold," Isaac murmured. "Chills. We need to scout out more wood."

I knew warmth wasn't the only reason Isaac wanted to keep the fire alive. With the flames dancing high, light spread across the clearing for fifty feet or more. No one could sneak up on us if we preserved that ring of light. "I'll go," I said. "I saw some downed stuff when I got our mattresses."

"Thanks, Muscle."

I dragged back a six-foot chunk of log as thick as my thigh, along with smaller limbs. Judging by their weight, they were dry. I went out for more, and when I came back, Isaac was working over the first load with his hatchet, cutting and splitting. So I kept collecting. The work kept my mind off things. I thought of Grandpa and Legs, up in these mountains, unafraid.

"I think that'll do it," Isaac said finally.

Darkness grew deeper. The hills barely showed themselves. Isaac finished chopping. He sat on the dirt next to a tall stack of firewood and stared at Phoebe.

"She's feverish," he said. "I gave her aspirin, but we need to get more fluids into her, and we're getting low on water." He held up a small metal cup in the firelight. "This is all we have left."

"I'll go back to the stream," I said, although I didn't want to. The thought of heading off by myself through a dark forest full of wild animals and who knew what else gave me the spinal willies.

"You're a trouper," Isaac said. "But you've already done your share. If you'd feel okay staying with her, I'll go."

What would I do if she got worse while Isaac was gone?

I touched her forehead. It was putting out heat like a furnace.

"I'm gone," I said, retying my shoelaces. I rummaged through my backpack, found my headlamp, and put it on. The bright beam helped me locate our three canteens (all empty) and check my watch (10:17). I hung one canteen from my belt; the others fit nicely in my hands.

"Stick to the trail, Russell," Isaac said. "If you think you've lost it, and you're not sure how to get back to it, stay put. If you're not back in an hour, I'll come and get you."

"I won't get lost." All we needed was for something else to go wrong.

"And keep your eyes open," he continued. "If Full Moon's back there, he'll see you coming before you see him."

I nodded, a bit of a lump in my throat. Isaac gave my shoulder a squeeze, and I took off at a jog. "Be quick," he said to my back.

The path was rough in places, crisscrossed by roots, booby-trapped by sticker vines and ankle-twisting plants, and littered with fallen branches. But moving without my pack felt good, and with the headlamp's beam bobbing in front of me, I didn't have a problem staying with the trail.

Phoebe needed water, in a hurry. No way was it going to take me an hour to get back. I was a runner, after all. I had speed. I had stamina.

Fifteen minutes later, breathing hard, I reached the

stream. My T-shirt and shorts were sticky with sweat. I knelt, gulping in the smells of woods and fast-moving water, and filled the canteens. I splashed water on a long sticker-bush gash on my leg and wiped off the dried blood. When I stood, my calf muscle complained a little, but I ignored it and started back.

A bright border of moon suddenly emerged above the mountaintops to the east, and as the big yellow globe—it was full tonight—rose higher, the path came alive with light. I switched off my headlamp. Now I could see, but I wouldn't *be* seen. Not as easily, anyway.

"Russell?" Isaac called as I approached the campsite at full tilt.

"Yeah," I grunted. As I slowed to a jog, my leg stopped nagging. The fire was still flaming high. Phoebe was still lying down. Isaac looked glad to see me. I handed him two of the canteens.

He whistled. "Thirty-one minutes. That's gotta be some kind of world record."

"How is she?" I said, in between breaths.

"The same. I just gave her the last of the water. You're a lifesaver, man."

I knelt down by Phoebe while Isaac began purifying the water. She opened her eyes and looked at me. After a moment she raised her hand and pointed at her eye in her nice-to-see-you gesture, and I returned it. She smiled.

"This stinks," I said a while later as Isaac and I sat by

the fire. He'd just forced more water on Phoebe, and she'd dozed off again.

"Yeah," Isaac said. "But now we're up here, close. Almost to where Legs wanted to be. Going ahead makes as much sense as going back, although Phoebe's not in shape for either."

"What about tomorrow?"

"I shouldn't have brought her up here," he said, ignoring my question, and for a moment that lost look came over his face. He looked younger and older at the same time.

"You couldn't have kept her away."

"Can you take the first watch?" he said. "I quit the pills, but my body still wants its sleep. If you wake me at two, you can have the rest of the night off."

"Sure." I wanted him to rest. He needed to be okay.

"Keep the fire blazing," he said, crawling into his bag. "Keep your eyes peeled. Wake Phoebs in an hour, then an hour and a half after that. Get her some water. Aspirin the second time. Get her to drink. Feel her head now and when you wake her. If she's hotter, if you see or hear anything, wake me."

"Okay."

"You're a good man, Muscle," Isaac said, and I felt the air grow warmer. I'd never figured out exactly what Isaac thought of me. Phoebe's little friend? Pest? Okay guy? I'd settle for *good man.*

He turned away. His breathing evened out and

deepened. I felt Phoebe's warm forehead with the back of my hand, then scooted closer to the fire. The sweat had cooled on my skin and shirt, and I was beginning to feel the chill of the night.

I threw another piece of wood on the fire, then got up and draped my sleeping bag around my shoulders like some ancient robed traveler—Aragorn, maybe. I pulled the bag over my head like a hood. Gandalf, on the lookout for orcs.

If the orc was out there, was he waiting for everyone to go to sleep? He'd have a long wait. Legs sore, calf stiff, I circled the campfire at a slug's pace, keeping my eyes on the trees. Once, twice, three times.

I bent and checked Phoebe's head. Warm but not warmer. I checked the time: 11:32. Time was crawling. Two-and-a-half crawling hours to go.

At midnight I woke Phoebe for water. She drank thirstily, and I had to tell her to take it easy. I didn't want it coming back on her.

The night slowly wore on. I sat till I felt sleepy then walked till I felt awake. I wanted coffee but didn't want to use water.

I woke Phoebe again at 1:30. She drank. She swallowed aspirin. Her forehead felt a little warmer, maybe, but I thought it was because my hands were cold now. She thought so, too. So I let Isaac sleep. I let him sleep till 2:00, then 2:30. He'd barely slept the night before.

I gave Phoebe more water at 2:45, finally waking Isaac at 3:00. "Time got away from me," I said.

"Thanks, man," he said. "How is she?"

"The same, I think. Feel her head."

He crouched barefoot next to Phoebe. He held his hand to her forehead. I laid another piece of wood on the fire, keeping an eye on her, watching her sleeping bag rise and fall.

"The same," Isaac said finally. "Get some sleep, Muscle. I've got the watch now." He stood and pulled on a sweatshirt and moved off to the edge of the circle of light.

I crawled into my sleeping bag, thinking that I wasn't sleepy, that this was a waste. But a moment later I drifted off.

Chapter Twenty-One

Jump:
July 29, Present

In my dream Legs is healthy and eagle-eyed, and he's leading the way up a trail, swinging a machete. Isaac is right behind him, walking tall and strong, then me. Phoebe is behind us somewhere; I can hear her humming along to her music.

A boiling cloud passes in front of the sun, bringing dark. Legs stumbles and falls and the machete skids into the undergrowth. Isaac helps him to his feet, but when Legs turns, his face is different, his whole body is different. And Isaac isn't helping him now, he's struggling with him. The Legs-guy dives to the ground and grabs the machete, but he's no longer the Legs-guy. He's wider, pig-faced. In the light and shadow of flames he looks like the devil's apprentice. He looks like Full Moon.

I tell myself to wake up. I force myself awake.

But the nightmare doesn't end. The flames are still there. And across the fire, Isaac and Full Moon are faced off, six feet apart. In Full Moon's hand is the machete.

"The map," Full Moon grunted. "Give me my brother's map. Then you kiddies can go home. No hard feelings."

Half-awake, I grabbed a five-foot chunk of branch, thick at one end. I rolled out of my bag and stood. I had to do something. At my feet, Phoebe lifted her head.

"Stay there, Muscle," Isaac said, pulling the hunting knife from his belt.

Full Moon snorted. His hand slipped inside his jacket and back out, smooth like butter. In the flickering light I wasn't sure what was in it. I prayed my first guess was wrong. But Pig-face brought his hand up, leveling it at Isaac. And in it was a pistol, big and dark. He tossed the machete away.

"What's going on?" Phoebe said dreamily.

"Okay." Isaac lowered the knife. "The map's not worth it."

"You're a smart kid." Sandpaper-in-pipe voice. Spine-freezing.

"I'll get it for you." Isaac groped through his backpack, keeping both eyes on Full Moon, who inched closer.

"Got it," Isaac said. Would he just hand it over? What choice did he have?

He held out the map to Full Moon, who snatched it away. "Thanks, hero." He backed off a few feet, and for a foolish moment I thought-hoped-prayed the nightmare was leaving. "You're the only ones left that know about this map. About the meteorite, even. Your parents wouldn't have let you go if they knew what you was after."

"My mom knows," I lied.

"No, she don't."

The knot around my insides grew tighter. "Legs will remember," Isaac said.

Full Moon spat. "The last time I saw Legs Leland, he looked like he wasn't gonna be helping anybody," he said. "The only thing he's gonna remember is the road to hell."

"You were in his room?" Isaac said.

"I was looking for what's mine. He woke up. The pillow shut him up. But no one's gonna find out." Full Moon kicked a piece of wood into the fire and it flared up, lighting his face. "You babies are gonna do something for me," he said. "You're gonna head over there." He kept the gun pointed at Isaac but gestured toward the cliff with his empty hand. "Now."

"If we don't?" Isaac said.

"Don't ask."

Phoebe struggled to her feet. "She's sick, man," Isaac said.

"She'll feel better soon." Full Moon waved the gun in the direction of the chasm. "Drop the knife. *Move.*"

Isaac dropped the knife. Holding Phoebe's arm, he started toward the place where darkness ended and blackness began. I took her other arm. She was trembling. Were we really going along with this? Part of me wanted to run, to take my chances on bullets in the dark. But I was paralyzed with fear. And I couldn't leave Phoebe and Isaac, no matter what.

We stopped three or four feet from the edge and turned to face Full Moon. I dropped my useless branch to the ground. Isaac positioned himself in front of Phoebe and me. A shield. "How'd you find us?" Isaac said. What difference did it make? I wondered. Then I realized he was stalling.

Full Moon wheezed with contempt. "I've been in and out of these hills my whole life. I've tracked deer and bear and lion, critters that barely leave a trace. You think it was hard tracking you? The last few miles, I could've just followed your *smell*." Even in the dim firelight, I could make out his familiar gap-toothed grin. I wanted to wipe it off his face.

His gaze shifted to the cliff. "I didn't get a chance to look in the daylight, but something tells me there's a lot of space out there before you get to anything solid. I'd like you guys to test it for me."

"*Jump?*" I said. I could barely get the word out.

"I could shoot you and dump you over. But that wouldn't look like an accident."

"You'll have to push us," Isaac said. "You can't expect us to jump."

"You asked for it, hero." Full Moon picked up my branch and held it in the crook of his left arm, fat end against his shoulder like a rifle butt. The gun stayed in his right hand. "Back up."

Isaac moved back and to his left, herding Phoebe and me along. I sensed the canyon yawning behind me. I could think of only one sickening thing: being shoved off into that black nothingness.

"You first, role model." Pig-face moved the pointy end of the branch up to Isaac's chest. "Say a prayer."

Chapter Twenty-Two

Last Dance:
July 29, Present

Full Moon thrust with all his weight.

But Isaac was ready. He twisted sideways. The tip of the branch slid off his chest. For an instant the big man was off balance, and an instant was all Isaac needed. He grabbed the limb and wrenched. Staggering forward, Full Moon dropped the branch and raised the gun.

Too late. Isaac grabbed Full Moon's wrist with both hands and held on, directing the muzzle away. But the man wrapped his free arm around Isaac's neck in a chokehold.

Isaac struggled against the thick forearm at his throat. "Run!" he gasped. "Home!"

Neither of us ran for home. "The machete!" Phoebe croaked. She dropped to her knees and began feeling around in the dim firelight. I grabbed the branch and moved toward Full Moon, looking for an opening. But the big man swung Isaac between us, aiming the pistol at me.

In one motion Isaac dropped his head and shoulders and flexed his knees. He planted his bare feet and pushed back against Full Moon's chest and gut. Back, toward the cliff. He staggered, with Isaac locked against him.

Isaac planted and pushed again. Full Moon took one awkward step, then another. In the next instant he was going over, leaning, dropping. But he didn't let go of Isaac. The big man held on as if he were holding onto a lifeline. His gun hand, empty now, flew up, grasping, but there was nothing to grasp. He was horizontal, flat out over the chasm, dragging Isaac with him like an anchor dragging a rope into the deep.

All I heard was the rattle of gravel, a thud, what might have been a gasp. Then nothing.

Phoebe's mouth was open in a silent scream.

I raced to the cliff. Suddenly, I remembered something. "He moved us over," I said. "When Full Moon was forcing us to the edge, Isaac *moved us over.*"

Phoebe staggered to her feet. "Moved us over?"

"When it was still light, I saw a ledge," I said.

I found a flashlight and pressed myself to the dirt, peering into the depths. Phoebe lay down beside me while I switched on the flashlight and directed its beam down, moving it deliberately left to right along the face of the cliff. She clutched my hand.

A sound—a moan—rose from somewhere below. Then a string of swear words, rapid-fire. The beam reached the spot where a ledge began angling out. Ten feet down, about.

"But here I am, at least," a voice said. "Alive. Still dodging bullets." I knew the voice. It wasn't a high-pitched wheeze. It was low and friendly and sounded like music.

I jerked the flashlight toward the sound.

Isaac pushed himself up to a sitting position with one arm. Holding his other arm close to his side, he leaned against the cliff face and looked up into the light. "Hi, Phoebs," he said. "Muscle."

"Full Moon?" My throat felt pinched. "He went over?"

"Highway to hell," Isaac said. "Almost took me with him."

I shuddered. I tried to think of how to help Isaac, but my brain was full of one image: Full Moon, tumbling through the night air. The picture should have made me happy, but it didn't. I felt empty and sick.

I took a deep breath, and another. I closed my eyes and tried to picture Grandpa's face.

I opened them. How could I help Isaac? I studied his perch. Narrow. Rocky. "We need to get you up."

"I messed up my shoulder," he said. "Separated, I think."

"We can do it," Phoebe said. But I wasn't sure how she'd help. She was barely able to crawl.

"The rope's in my pack." Isaac's words came out strained, as if he'd hurt more than his shoulder.

I found the rope and hurried back. I tried not to think about Full Moon lying at the bottom of this cliff. Was he *dead?*

Phoebe held the flashlight while I began playing out one end of the rope.

"Secure the other end," Isaac said. "Something sturdy. A stump. A log." His words came out in bursts. "A big rock. I don't want to pull you over."

I went back to the campsite, found another flashlight, and searched for an anchor. It took me only a moment to find a thick stump thirty feet from the cliff. It had enough bumps and knobs that the rope, once fastened, wouldn't be likely to ride up and over. "Got something," I called. I got busy, wrapping the rope around the stump, knotting it tight.

I went back to the cliff and knelt next to Phoebe. Isaac had looped the rope around his right wrist and was sitting, staring out. "How's that gonna work?" Phoebe said.

"I need you to perform a little adjustment first."

"An adjustment?" I said.

"I wanna see if you two can pull my arm back into joint. Before you try to get me up. I could give you more help that way."

My stomach turned over as I imagined Isaac's arm popping back into its socket.

"We'll try." Phoebe's voice sounded feeble but hopeful.

"Good," Isaac said. "How's your knot, Muscle?"

"Guaranteed to hold 150 pounds," I said. "What do you weigh?"

"About 170."

"Just right," I said, and Isaac gave a weak laugh.

"Go check out the knot," I told Phoebe. "How the rope looks."

She went to the stump. "Sturdy," she said when she returned. She lay down and peeked over.

Down on the ledge, Isaac was on his back, using his left hand to hold his right arm in the air. His face was twisted with pain and effort. "Okay," he said. "Both of you move away from the edge. Grab a section of rope and crouch down. You'll get more leverage that way. Take in the rope until there's no slack. When I say go, you need to start applying steady pressure until I tell you to stop."

Phoebe made a small noise in her throat.

"Okay?" Isaac said.

"Okay," I said. We backed away, grabbed the rope, and crouched, Phoebe in front of me. We took in the slack.

"Ready?" Isaac said.

"Ready," we said in one breath.

"Set," Isaac said. "Go!"

We pulled, together and steady, and Isaac let out a moan, then a stream of profanity. "Keep going," he gasped. His voice sounded empty.

"We will," Phoebe said. In the next instant, though, I heard her retching and gagging. But she was still tugging steadily. "I'm fine," she said to me, almost drowning out the sound of Isaac's groans.

Why were we doing this? It was too much for Phoebe, too much for Isaac. Maybe we could haul him up and then mess with his shoulder. Or get him back to civilization and let a doctor fix it. I could run ahead for help, even.

But we kept applying pressure. Finally we heard Isaac again: a moan, a sigh, then, "Stop."

We went to the cliff edge.

"How about dropping me a flashlight?" Isaac said. He was standing, smiling up at us. Both of his hands were in the air. "I need to check out the face of this cliff."

"We did it?" I dropped my flashlight and Isaac caught it.

"You did it," Isaac said. "My shoulder's pretty sore, but in place. You doctors do good work."

"Get that rope around you," Phoebe said.

"Will do." Isaac wrapped and looped and knotted the rope around his chest, fashioning a harness. He played the flashlight beam across the cliff wall. "There's a few hand holds above me here," he said, "which should make it easier for us." He tugged the rope. "Make sure the line rides on something smooth once I'm off the ground. Dirt or grass or slick rock—something that won't slice or dice."

"Okay," I said. What would happen if the rope gave way with Isaac dangling from it? There was no guarantee he'd end up on the ledge again. I backed up a few feet, taking the slack out of the line, while Phoebe maneuvered its contact point to a channel of soft dirt between two rock outcroppings.

"Ready?" I said.

"When you are," Isaac called.

"Let's move back before we start pulling," Phoebe said to me. "When we gain rope, we can wrap it around the stump to keep it from slipping back."

"Thinking all the time," I said.

We stepped back, letting the rope run through our fingers, keeping it taut. Four feet from the stump we stopped and crouched.

"Now!" Phoebe said.

The rope tightened but for a long moment there was no progress. Then it gave, and moved. A few inches, then more. We took a step back and dug in.

"Now!" Isaac said, and we pulled hard and gained more rope. For an instant it went just a little slack and we leaned back.

"That's it," Isaac grunted. "Keep it tight when I move to a different hold."

We pulled again. I pictured Isaac scaling the wall like Spiderman. While I held on, Phoebe circled the slack around the stump and set the flashlight on top of it, aimed toward the cliff. Then she rejoined me.

"Halfway there!" Isaac called out. "More than halfway, maybe!"

His words felt like a gift. But we gave another pull and nothing happened.

"Hold on," Isaac said. "I'm looking for another hold."

We waited, maintaining tension. "Now!" Isaac said, and we pulled and gained ground. "Now!" We gained more. Phoebe looped more rope around the trunk.

"Now!" Isaac said, and suddenly in the beam of the flashlight one hand materialized, then another.

"Now!" Isaac said again, and his face—a dirty mask of pain and effort—rose above the cliff edge.

Isaac hung on and let us work, and his shoulders appeared, then his trunk, his legs. As he came over he twisted onto his back. When the rescue team finally stopped tugging, he lay spread-eagled, staring up at the stars.

We dropped the rope and helped him to his feet. He hugged us, long, then wobbled to the fire and sat. Phoebe dropped beside him and clung to him like a coat of paint.

Chapter Twenty-Three
James and Matthew: October 9, 1865

The tall, thin passenger with the wispy beard wasn't what James had pictured. He hung back, confused. But his mother ran to the man across the wet, slippery boards of the dock and embraced him, burying her head in the loose lapels of the tattered overcoat that hung from his shoulders like a drape.

James, still unsure, inched closer, studying the man's face as he took off his stained, wide-brimmed hat and revealed a ragged purplish scar running eyebrow to ear top along the left side of his head. There was no recognition in his eyes as his arms went around his mother, as he looked up at James's cautious approach. They were Matthew's eyes nonetheless; beneath a nose knocked crooked, the mouth was his. But the smile James remembered was gone.

Tears flowed down his mother's face. "Matthew, we missed you so," she said, but Matthew said nothing. He only held on tighter, stared at James, let the hat drop to the dock. He breathed in deep, as if savoring his mother's smell.

Does he know me? James wondered. "I'm *James*," he said, and eyed his brother's face, trying to look inside that tortured skin, that battered bone. Nothing. How could James talk to this shadow of his brother? If James broke the news of Dr. Evans's death, would Matthew even recognize the name? Would he understand Dr. Jackson's story? Who would answer all of James's carefully preserved questions?

"James," Matthew said, but it was only a word. Like *mother* and *mountain* and *meteorite*. Something from an old and elusive dream.

James went to Matthew and put his arms around him, holding on tight, trying desperately to draw him back from wherever he'd gone.

Chapter Twenty-Four

Solo:
July 29, Present

We all drank our fill of water. I'd never tasted anything so sweet. Then I left Isaac and Phoebe, with him trying to get her to eat some apple and cracker, and her telling him that he wasn't her mother. We needed more wood, and finding it was my specialty.

I should have been tired, but I'd never felt more awake in my life. The night air was thick with the wonderful smells and sounds of living things—fir trees, wildflowers, leaves rustling on high branches, small furry bodies scuttling through low undergrowth.

I'd just made it through most of a night I would never forget. And Isaac was alive. Isaac had saved us and then needed saving himself, and Phoebe and I had been up to it. We'd done it.

And Full Moon was gone.

"How are you guys feeling?" I said when I got back.

"Fine," Phoebe said, but her face still had that bleached, hollow look.

"Better," Isaac said. "I shouldn't have trusted myself to sit. I nodded off, and Full Moon snuck up on me."

"His mistake," I said, trying to convince myself that Full Moon had deserved to die. He tried to kill Legs. He tried to kill us. I was thankful that he wouldn't be around to terrorize us again.

But I hated that he was dead, that he had had no chance for redemption, that I'd seen him take his last awkward step into eternity. Or oblivion. It was horrible.

For a long time we all just stared into the fire. I looked into Phoebe's eyes and saw my emotions mirrored there. Isaac's eyes were clouded; his face was unreadable.

A layer of clouds hid the hilltops when I woke in the morning. But the sun was up, I could tell that much. I blinked sleep out of my eyes and focused on my watch: 7:40. Not exactly an early start on the day, but still I was tempted to stay in my sleeping bag.

Until I thought about the meteorite. Until I thought about the events of the night before. Until I saw Phoebe still in her bag, breathing deep and easy, and Isaac sitting near the edge of the cliff.

I lurched to my feet and walked barefoot over to him and sat. "It wasn't a dream. He's really dead, right?"

"He's dead," Isaac said. "Down there somewhere, out of

sight. That makes it easier to take. But he's still dead." He studied my face. "You're a brave kid, Muscle."

"When he had the gun pointed at us and we were at the edge of the cliff, I almost peed my pants."

"Good," Isaac said. "If you're not scared, you're not human. You forget how to treat other humans."

"Were you? Scared, I mean?"

"Enough. I've seen death before—too much of it. My shrink says I need to focus on life. I'm trying, but this isn't going to help." He twisted to gaze out over the valley. The leg of his jeans rode up above his ankle.

The sheath was there, empty. Where was the knife?

Had Full Moon really missed the ledge and kept going?

Or did he have help?

"Do we have to tell the cops when we get back?" I said. What if they found Full Moon with a knife in his ribs? What would happen to Isaac? Would speeding-ticket experts be able to recognize self-defense when they saw it?

"They'll have to be told what Full Moon admitted about Legs, what he tried to do to us, the whole story. Someone will have to come up here and look for the body." I was glad Isaac didn't seem concerned about the police.

"What's going on?" Phoebe's voice. Still pale, she was up on one elbow, staring at us.

"Nothing, Phoebs." Isaac got up and headed toward her with a slight limp, holding his shoulders stiff. "How're you feeling?"

"Better, maybe." She was still trying to sound cheerful. "I'll see when I stand up."

Isaac helped her to her feet. She clung to his arm, hunched over, and I knew she wouldn't be going anywhere soon. But we had to. We couldn't return to Grandpa and Legs with nothing but almosts and shoulda-couldas and excuses.

"We gotta get going," Phoebe said. "We're behind schedule."

Isaac frowned. "We need to talk." He helped her sit.

"I'm the only healthy one," I said. "I'll go on, let you guys rest."

Phoebe shook her head. "I'm fine," she said.

"I promised your mom, Muscle," Isaac said, "that I'd keep an eye on you."

"We're almost there," I said. "What else could go wrong?"

Isaac raised his eyebrows. *Lots of things,* his expression said. And maybe he was right. But Legs wouldn't worry about possible maybes. Neither would Grandpa.

"You gotta let me go," I said. "Otherwise this was all a waste."

"You trying to be a hero, Muscle?"

"How would Legs feel if we came home empty-handed?" I said.

"We have to recognize an ugly possibility," Isaac said. "Legs could be dead."

"He's *not*," Phoebe said.

"He's tough," I said.

"I hope he's alive," Isaac said.

"There's no map," Phoebe said. "How could you find the meteorite all by yourself without even a map?"

"That *would* be a problem," Isaac said, but there was a twinkle in his eyes. He tugged off his shoe. He pulled out a wrinkled piece of paper and slowly unfolded it.

The map.

I could barely believe it. "What did you give Full Moon?"

"A counterfeit I'd made up, just in case. I hoped he'd take it and leave." He grinned. "He would've ended up in California."

"So I can go?" I said.

"We *all* can go," Phoebe said.

"Sorry, Phoebs," Isaac said.

"What if I get better?"

"Then maybe we'll meet up with Russell on his way back." Isaac's words sank in. *He was going to let me do it.* I grinned. Isaac handed me the map.

Phoebe leaned back against a log and closed her eyes. "He'll be all alone."

"So he's gotta be extra careful," Isaac said. "But we'll give him the stuff to keep him safe and on track."

A half-hour later, I was ready, weighed down with

enough for an overnight. Just in case I couldn't get back before dark.

"One more thing." Isaac went to his pack, rummaged through it, and brought out a battered metal saltshaker. He unscrewed the lid and took out a tiny manila envelope, sealed. "Legs gave me this," he said, handing it to me. "He said to open this envelope when we get to the point where we're ready to leave the bike trail. He said to keep it somewhere safe and separate from the map."

I stuffed it carefully into my backpack. I patted my shirt pocket to make sure the map was there.

Phoebe stood and gave me a hug. It wasn't embarrassing; it felt just right. "Be careful," she said. She reached into her pack, took out her music player, and gave it to me.

"Thanks," I said. "I'll take good care of it."

"Be smart," Isaac said. "I'll be a *real* mess if something happens to you." He took me by the shoulders and looked me in the eye. "Okay?"

"Okay." I headed across the clearing to pick up the trail. When I found the entrance—a wide space between two old-growth stumps—I turned and waved. Isaac and Phoebe, small in the distance, sat on a log with smoke curling up behind them. They waved back.

Chapter Twenty-Five
Legs's Secret:
July 29, Present

Fifty feet into the thick woods the light faded, but the trail was clear. I thought of the map, of what I had to do. Somewhere between three and six miles on the trail, then the marker, a tombstone-shaped block of stone. There I was supposed to cut off the trail to my right, heading southeast, with only the compass, a creek, and some landmarks—hills and ridges and finally the bald mountain itself, its broken face, the day-glo backpack Legs had left so long ago—to show me the way.

I turned on Phoebe's music, tried to get into a walking rhythm, and checked the time: 9:10. Time would be important. It would tell me how far I'd gone, how far I had to go, whether I'd be able to do it in one day or spend the night. I walked faster, building up a sweat.

The trail left the high ridge and headed down and then up again, between two hills, curling around the back of one, still heading southeast. It rose out of the trees and into sunlight. To the left was a steep drop and bare rock. To the right was the face of the hill, treed, but marked with fallen timber and wedges of gray and brown where dirt and rocks had broken loose.

I slowed, eyes down, making sure of my footing. I didn't want to stumble off and go over like an uprooted tree. Or Full Moon.

I rounded a bend and the trail ended, wiped out by a slide.

Now what? I could double back and try another approach. But once I got off this trail, my chances of getting lost would skyrocket.

Or I could scramble across the slide, hoping I didn't start a new one and end up buried halfway down the mountain.

Isaac had said be careful. But Isaac wouldn't turn back. I was sure of it. I backtracked until I found a stout branch to use as a walking stick. I turned off the music and stowed the player in my pack. I needed to concentrate.

The dirt compressed as I moved ahead, planting the stick on the downslope, keeping my weight distributed. I estimated the distance to where the trail resumed again. A hundred feet, maybe.

I covered ten of it, twenty, thirty. I took one more step, just like the rest.

Without warning, the ground gave way. My foot slipped, dropping me hard to my right knee. A cascade of small rocks rattled down the hill. But I leaned on the limb, fighting to stay upright.

And I did. I eased back to my feet, calf twinging, heart pounding, and continued on, slower, testing my foot plants before putting down my full weight. Fifty feet, seventy-five. Twenty to go, then ten.

Then I was there. Solid ground. I took one look back, breathed deep, and went on.

The trail continued along the side of the hill—southwest, according to the compass—then switched back and down, heading northeast again. The ground flattened out, trees thickened, undergrowth crept out over the trail.

I got out the machete and hacked my way through branches and sticker vines and tangles of fallen growth. The going got slower, but I tried to stay on a pace and keep track of how much ground I was covering.

The sun rose higher, I dripped sweat, my shoulders and back ached, my calf felt tight. I stopped and drank, downed an apple, checked my watch, the map, the compass. I was doing okay: on course, maybe on time. I should be getting close to the cutoff point.

I kept at it. Walking and hacking, crawling over and under, walking and hacking. I heard running water and stopped. Off to my left, exactly where it should be. Up ahead, the trail would cross the creek over a bridge heading east. Then the rock, the turnoff to the southeast, and the great unmarked unknown.

The sound of the water grew louder. I could smell it, then see it through the trees, down an embankment, thirty feet away. I shrugged off my backpack and made my way to the stream. I knelt and splashed the icy water on my face and arms, doused my hair. None in my mouth.

I got to my feet, staring at the dancing water, the smooth, green-bearded rocks, wondering how Phoebe was doing. I wished she and Isaac were with me.

The trail wound through trees, following the stream, then opened up onto a small clearing. I worked my way through another stand of trees and came to the bridge, which turned out to be nothing but a huge log, five feet thick and fifty or more feet in length, easily long enough to span the creek bed. The log had been sawed flat on the top surface, but it looked slick with moss and moisture. A rickety railing made of thin logs was spiked to one side, my left. I tested it as I stepped on. Stronger than it looked, but I'd use it only for balance.

Cautiously I started off, glancing down. Water and rocks. Fifteen feet below. Not where I wanted to go.

Halfway across, my leg tightened. I took a cautious step, testing, then a long stride, stretching.

My shoe slid on the slime; then screaming at me in a full-scale cramp, my calf bunched up. I jerked my weight off it, bent to grab it, and slipped on the mossy surface. Off balance, I reached for the railing, but I was going the other way, too fast. Before I could think, I was below the log, falling headfirst toward the rushing water.

Arms down! I told myself. *Arms down!*

I hit and went under—hands, arms, head, body. Freezing water. Brain-chilling. Tumbling. But no rocks. I went all the way to the bottom—sand and smooth stones—and almost righted myself before the current drove my shoulder against my first real rock, a big boulder that bounced me out of the main flow.

My head cleared the surface. I could breathe. My feet touched. But now my backpack was caught in the current, threatening to drag me downstream. I shrugged it off, grabbed a strap, and backpedaled toward shore, towing it.

I got to dry land. I sat, dripping and cold, but glad to be alive and in one piece. My shoulder was sore, but everything else, even my nuisance of a calf, felt okay.

I looked up. The bridge was silhouetted against trees and sky, not more than fifty feet upstream. I hadn't traveled far, but I'd taken the tough route across the creek.

I emptied my shoes of water. I wrung out my socks. I let my backpack and sleeping bag dribble onto the sand while I checked the flaps and pockets to be sure nothing had come loose. Everything looked secure.

I remembered the map.

My hand flew to my shirt pocket. Empty. I got up and searched the shoreline, upstream and down. Nothing. I paced, dripping, picturing the map. I'd already covered most of its twists and turns and ups and downs and overs and throughs. There wasn't much left. I thought I could recall the rest of it, even with a flash-frozen brain.

I'd had a little setback, I was a little wet, but so what? Isaac wouldn't be stopped by something like this. Phoebe would pretend she'd enjoyed the refreshing dip. Grandpa would barely notice the interruption. And Legs would already be back on the trail, tracking his meteorite.

I would keep going.

I struggled into my socks and shoes, shouldered my drenched, noticeably heavier pack, walked back along the shoreline and climbed the bank where the bridge met it. I concentrated on the woods to my right, where the rock was supposed to be. Thirty seconds passed. A minute. The marker had looked close on the map; the turnoff would have to be nearby.

I glimpsed something through the trees. A gray-green slab of rock angling out of the ground. The tombstone.

I eased my pack to the ground and got out a piece of bread and a chunk of cheese. A little squashed, but dry inside plastic bags. I checked my watch. Almost eleven. I found a sunny spot to sit, and washed down the food with warm water. Then I remembered the little envelope. Open it at the turnoff, Isaac had told me.

I pulled the soggy envelope from my backpack and carefully sliced it open. Inside was a wet piece of paper, folded and folded again. It smelled musty. I opened it carefully to keep it from tearing.

Luckily, the ink hadn't run. At the top were two words: MAP AMENDMENT. Legs's handwriting. Below the words was another map—smaller but just as detailed—and more words. DISREGARD FIRST MAP FROM THIS POINT ON, it said in the space between the log bridge and an X labeled TOMBSTONE-SHAPED ROCK. Starting at the X and heading away from the stream toward the northeast was a line, labeled here and there with landmarks.

The real route to the meteorite.

Legs had taken no chances. If someone—Full Moon, for instance—had gotten his hands on the first map, he would've come within five miles and then wandered off on a wild goose chase. The first map was worthless without the second. And Legs had kept them separate. And secret. Even Isaac didn't know what was in the little envelope. No one did.

Except me.

I studied the new map. The route looked no more difficult than the bogus one, except there would be no stream to follow, nothing to keep me on course but landmarks and my compass. With the sun high in the sky, counting on my sense of direction would be a mistake.

I buttoned up the map in a cargo pocket of my shorts, strapped on my pack, picked out an opening in the trees, and set off.

An hour passed. My clothes were drying off a little. I

was making better time than I'd expected. Most of the time I'd been able to keep the machete in my backpack and my eyes on the compass. And I'd found my first landmark—a beaver pond—with help. One of the residents, sensing my approach, had tail-slapped a warning. Otherwise, off track by then, I would have wasted time searching.

But I'd located the pond, shouted an echoing, "Thanks, beav!" to a small dark head carving a V across the surface, and cut around to the east shore. From there I oriented myself with a sharp-peaked mountain in the northeast and kept going.

I worked toward the peak, keeping a pace, angling closer to the slope of a wooded hill on my right. I was to half-circle around to its back side. At that point, the round-shouldered mountain—Legs's mountain—should come into view.

I was moving across the hill's lower slopes when I came to a clearing. Now I could see past the north face of the hill, through a kind of valley.

And I saw a mountain, dome-shaped, standing by itself.

I stopped and stared, searching its face for a landmark— an open area, with the clump of trees in the middle Legs had described.

And then, through the wisps of a low cloud, it materialized. Not a clearing, exactly, but a circular area of different colors, different trees, much shorter than the others surrounding them. And in the middle of the clearing grew a taller stand of leafy trees. The curtain of birches from Legs's story? His oasis?

The weight on my back would slow me down. Next to a tall, limbless snag I could recognize when I returned, I stashed the stuff I wouldn't need on the mountain. Then I slipped my nearly-empty pack back on and double-timed across a meadow to the mountain's base.

I started up, struggling with thickening growth and the steepness of the slope. I could feel my heart thumping, sweat pooling under my already-soggy shirt.

I fought through one more thicket and broke out, into an expanse of dirt and spindly saplings and young evergreens and low-growing shrubs and rubble everywhere. In the middle of the once-upon-a-time clearing stood a cluster of taller trees. I headed for them. This was what Legs had described; this was where I'd find his orange backpack, propped against a tree.

Above me, the ground was strewn with fractured boulders and rocks and cinders and downed timber, charred and crumbling. But I didn't see the backpack, even as I struggled within seventy-five yards, then fifty, of the bigger trees. And my heart drummed doubt into my head. Maybe this wasn't the right clearing. Maybe I'd gotten off course between where I'd left my stuff and here. Maybe it wasn't even the right mountain.

But I pushed myself ahead, eyes probing the ground.

Didn't this *have* to be the right place? A clump of trees in the middle of a steep-sloped former clearing on a round mountain? The trees were bigger than I'd imagined, but after a century and a half, wouldn't they finally be coming back strong?

I took a step, then two, into the stand of trees.

From somewhere overhead, a bird called out an alarm.

I looked up through the leaves and spotted something. It looked like a patch of orange cloth, shaded and shadowed by the thick growth all around it.

My heart, already thumping in my chest from the climb, picked up its pace. I located a slender tree trunk below the orange.

I hoisted myself up to one branch, then another. The cloth was still out of reach. I boosted myself up one more limb, stood, held on, leaned out, and groped blindly for an object that didn't belong.

Nothing, nothing, then something. Cloth. A pack, empty. I tugged until I could reach a buckle, then pressed and pulled and pushed until I felt it click and open. I pulled at the cloth again. It resisted, then came free, and suddenly I had it, close up, inches from my face.

A backpack. Day-glo orange once, now dimmed. But the one Legs had talked about. The young tree must have sprouted up underneath it and carried it skyward.

This was the place.

Chapter Twenty-Six

Eyeball:
July 29, Present

Iscrambled down, dropped the old faded pack, and started through the trees at a jog. When I reached the other side, I looked up at the face of the slope and remembered what Legs had said—that the upcropping looked like someone had taken a bite out of it. I saw that, but to me it looked more like a half-finished sculpture: a nose, an empty eye socket on one side, and on the other, an eyeball, big and round and half-buried in the mountainside.

Legs's meteorite.

I climbed up to it slowly. I knew it wasn't going anywhere, but I couldn't take my eyes off it as I got closer and it got bigger, more tangible.

Then I was there, reaching out, touching it, feeling its solid, immovable weight, the smooth-rough surface.

It was real. It was *real.*

It had traveled millions of miles through the dark emptiness of space to land here.

I circled it once, twice, taking it in. Then I pulled out my hammer and chisel. I looked for a protrusion, something I could chip away.

I found places where the surface was lighter-colored and irregular. Where it looked as if someone had split off something long before. Legs, maybe, but some were darker, older. Dr. Evans's work? I felt like a time traveler, arriving a hundred and fifty years in the past.

I took my time. Closing my eyes, I let my hands do the work. I pressed my cheek against the rock's surface and felt its texture, its coolness, imagining the near misses of its route through the heavens. Had someone or something on a distant planet seen this piece of the sky streak past centuries before and wondered where it was going?

My fingers brushed across a ridge and paused and re-crossed it, measuring its length and width, the depth of the furrows surrounding it. Not big but big enough; not deep but deep enough.

It would do.

I angled the chisel blade against the bump and brought the hammer down. Once. Again. Harder. Nothing.

I moved the blade a fraction of an inch, re-angled it, and tried again. The hammer hit and glanced off and rapped against my thumb, sending a jolt of pain up my arm to my brain. I swore—loud—and heard my voice echo off the hillsides as I raised the hammer and brought it down with a full charge of adrenaline.

It hit square. I felt something give at the same time a chunk of rock flew off and thudded into the soft dirt.

I picked it up, weighing it in my hand. It was only about the size of my sore thumb, but unusually heavy. Piece-of-the-sky heavy. Mantel-rock heavy. And the freshly fractured surface looked the same as the inside surface of the piece Legs had shown us.

I had my specimen.

I put the slice of rock in a small but deep pocket inside the main compartment of my backpack and snapped the outer flaps closed. Double-safe. Shouldering the pack, I started downhill. At the near edge of the stand of trees I turned and took a long look at Legs's meteorite.

At Matthew's meteorite.

I located the snag just as the sun dropped below a tall peak to the west. Lots of daylight remained, but night was on its way. It would come early to valleys and forests, bringing a chill to my damp clothes.

I picked up my gear and hurried on, feeling light on my feet and ready for anything. I'd done what Isaac and Phoebe had sent me to do. I had a chunk of magic in my pack.

I had Legs's treasure.

I had something to light a fire in Grandpa's eyes.

Chapter Twenty-Seven
Matthew: July 13, 1878

Matthew helped Ulysses scramble over the last driftwood log, then swung him down to the flat, uncluttered beach, where his short legs were more at home. Barefoot, he sprinted to the water, kicking up puffs of sand. He splashed in, squealing at the cold, while Matthew hurried stiff-legged after him.

"Careful now, Ulysses," he called. "Yesterday I saw a flatfish the size of a barn door here."

Ulysses high-stepped through the water, staring down, left and right. "I'm not afraid of any flatfish," he said. "I'll stand on his back. I'll ride him like a horse."

Matthew laughed at the bravery of his six-year-old son. It warmed Matthew's heart to laugh, to be able to laugh. He kicked off his boots and waded into the icy tide, smiling as Ulysses raced back and forth, searching for his mount. He was a gift, there was no other way to think of him, and Matthew was grateful for him, for the rest of his family, every waking and dreaming moment.

"Are you afraid, you big flatty?" Ulysses called, splashing deeper, peering into the blue-green-white. "Come be my pony."

"Are you numb yet, Ulysses?" Matthew's own feet had lost half their feeling. He looked down at them through the water, vaguely recalling other water, pink with blood.

"No flatties, Dad."

"I think you scared them off, son."

"Will you give me a ride?"

"To wherever you wish to go." Matthew swept him up and set him on his shoulders and giant-slogged through the low waves.

Ulysses chuckled at the bouncing. "The sun-catcher."

"Done." Matthew loped out of the water, through the hard, wet sand, up to the dry, where the storm-driven, sun-bleached corpse of a giant cedar rested well past the high tide mark.

Matthew lifted Ulysses over his head and set him on top of the log, then climbed up the ladder of roots to sit next to him, catching his breath. The sun felt wonderful, and they lay back, soaking it in. But soon Ulysses sprang up again, eyes sparkling, looking out at the sea. Matthew turned the opposite way, east, toward the mountains.

"Why do you always look off that way, Dad?"

Matthew's fingers danced over his scar and settled at his temple. He rubbed, trying to clear away the cobwebs. It was so hard to remember. He stared off at the hills, cloud-free, emerald-colored in the sunshine. They looked close enough to touch, but he knew how far off they were. He knew how difficult it would be to get there, to get through them. He knew something else. "Your Uncle James has a rock on his mantel," he said.

"He lets me hold it sometimes," Ulysses said.

"What does it feel like, Ulysses?"

"Heavy."

"It came from those hills," Matthew said. He nodded toward the round shoulders in the distance. "I brought it out, many years ago, James tells me. But before that it came from somewhere else, from as far away as the stars that shine at night."

"Really?" Ulysses looked up into the blue, as if he could see them.

"Someday you and I will hike into those hills, Ulysses."

"Can Mom and Sarah go with us?" He waved, and a hundred yards down the beach a woman and a small girl waved back. They were hurrying toward the big log, swinging a picnic basket between them.

Matthew smiled. "Of course. And Uncle James and Aunt Rose. We'll need their help. Somewhere up in those hills is another rock like the one you've held in your hand, but thousands of times bigger. Sometimes I hear it calling to me."

"Calling to you? A rock?"

"Not just a rock, Son. A piece of the sky."

Author's Note

The main characters in this story—Russell, Phoebe, Isaac, Legs, Art, Full Moon, Matthew, James, their families and acquaintances—are fictitious. But there really was a Dr. John Evans, a physician and amateur but well-regarded naturalist. He and two French-Canadian companions, employees of the Hudson's Bay Company, explored parts of the Oregon Territory, including a route from Port Orford to Eugene City, in 1856. Doctor Evans made a return trip to the Territory in 1858. Eventually, the doctor sent geologic samples from his expeditions to Dr. Charles Jackson, a well-respected scientist in Boston. One of the samples was determined to be a piece of meteorite by Dr. Jackson (and other experts who have examined it since).

Once his suspicions were confirmed, Dr. Evans revealed that the specimen had been chiseled from a huge, half-buried rock that he'd discovered on a bald mountain in the coastal range near Port Orford during his 1856 exploration. He described the mountain and its whereabouts in general terms and began to make plans to return to the area. But he had a hard time finding funding. The Civil War was approaching. Before he could return to Oregon, he fell ill and died.

Other scientists looked at Dr. Evans's records. They looked at his letters to Dr. Jackson in which he described the area of the discovery. Other expeditions were launched to find the meteorite. But Dr. Evans's notes lacked detail. They were missing maps and distances and directions. The landmarks were vague. There were many mountains that could be described as "bald." The scientists weren't able to locate the meteorite.

Since then, many others have tried. In the century and a half that has passed, numerous individuals and groups—professional and amateur—have attempted to find Dr. Evans's meteorite. They've had no luck.

But can anyone blame them—and future explorers—for trying? Although it's estimated that many tons of meteoroids ("space rocks") enter our atmosphere every day, only the larger pieces survive to make impact with Earth or sea and earn the name *meteorite.* And only a small percentage of these are seen or found. So a meteorite is a rarity, much rarer than gold and often more valuable to collectors, sometimes fetching a thousand dollars or more per ounce. Can you imagine what a ten-ton meteorite might be worth?

By the time most meteorites land on Earth, the wear and tear of space travel has reduced them to a relatively small size. But some monsters have entered our atmosphere and survived.

Close to home, about fifty thousand years ago, a meteorite fifty meters across blasted out Arizona's Barringer Crater, which is twelve hundred meters (about three quarters of a mile) in diameter and two hundred meters deep.

Another meteorite, sixty meters wide, touched down in Siberia in 1908 and flattened trees for thirty miles around the point of impact.

And researchers believe that sixty-five million years ago, a meteorite or asteroid *six miles in diameter* struck the Yucatán area of Mexico. This colossus created a crater a hundred miles wide. It rocketed so much terrestrial and extraterrestrial material high into the atmosphere that the earth's weather cooled dramatically, killing off half the species of animals in existence, including the last of the dinosaurs.

Yet there are scientists who doubt the authenticity of Dr. Evans's story. They feel he may have bought his specimen at the time of his second trip west, and that it is actually from a famous meteorite field in Chile known as Imilac, where pallasite meteorites as large as four hundred fifty pounds have been found. The sample bears a resemblance to other specimens from that field. The doctor didn't submit the specimen until after his second trip, and he needed funding for another expedition. What better way to raise interest (and money) than to promise the prestige and rewards of such a discovery to a potential investor? And why hasn't anyone been able to duplicate Dr. Evans's find?

But there are still many who believe a lost ten-ton

meteorite worth millions of dollars lies half-buried on the side of a mountain on Oregon's southern coast. Andrew M. Davis, a scientist who has studied both Dr. Evans's slice of meteorite and pieces from the field in South America where some suspect Dr. Evans's sample originated, has stated that the differences are greater than the similarities. In his opinion, based on his pallasite data base, Dr. Evans's specimen did not come from Imilac.

Perhaps we'll never know. But perhaps one day someone—maybe a young someone with more dreams than doubts—will venture into those green hills that rise above the blue Pacific. Perhaps that someone will struggle up the side of a round mountain, make a discovery, and recognize it for what it is—a piece of the sky.

About David Patneaude

When David Patneaude was a youngster, his favorite story was Robert Louis Stevenson's *Treasure Island,* a tale of adventure, suspense, mystery, and best of all, buried treasure.

David never found pirate plunder of his own, but now he digs for a different kind of hidden loot—story ideas. So he was doubly intrigued when he discovered a real-life account of, what else? Lost treasure. Then it was up to him to develop the idea, which is what writers often do—take a fragment of something that's happening (or has happened) around us and expand it into a story. *A Piece of the Sky,* David's eighth book with Albert Whitman, is the result.

David lives in Woodinville, Washington, with his wife, Judy, a junior-high-school librarian, and (sometimes) his daughter Jaime and son Jeff, college students, and not far from son Matt, daughter-in-law Arika, and twin grandsons Jasper and Kai.

Learn more about David at www.patneaude.com.